Midnight Kiss

by Jude Ouvrard

Midnight Kiss

Jude Ouvrard

This book is a work of fiction. Names, characters, places and incidents are products of the author's imagination and are not to be construed as real. Any resemblance to actual events, locales, organizations, or persons living or dead, is entirely coincidental.

COPYRIGHT

Trient Press

3375 S Rainbow Blvd

#81710, SMB 13135

Las Vegas,NV 89180

Ordering Information:

Quantity sales. Special discounts are available on quantity purchases by corporations, associations, and others. For details, contact the publisher at the address above.

Orders by U.S. trade bookstores and wholesalers. Please contact Trient Press: Tel: (775) 996-3844; or visit www.trientpress.com.

Printed in the United States of America

Publisher's Cataloging-in-Publication data

Ouvrard, Jude

A title of a book : Midnight Kiss

ISBN Hard Cover: 978-1-953975-86-7

Paperback: 978-1-953975-84-3

E-book: 978-1-953975-85-0

Prologue

Shy smile, pretty long blonde hair, she is my type of woman. Every time I see her at the Sweet Kisses bakery, I swear she blushes or is so bubbly she practically glows. Outside of the bakery, when she is with her husband, she's like a black and grey picture. No joy, barely a smile touches her face and her grey eyes hide so much. I don't know what her relationship is like but I know I could give her so much. I could bring back the color to her world.

I have one failed marriage behind me. And it made me realize what I want out of this life and she represents a huge part of it. For now though, all I can do is bring her a smile every few days when I get the guys a box of cupcakes and that's enough. For now. It has to be.

Chapter 1

After selling my wedding ring at the jeweller this morning, I feel pretty amazing. Free from the cage I was living in for so long. Freedom will be great, I can already feel it. My finger is a lot lighter now.

Knowing that I won't ever see this ring again is the best damn feeling. I loved Derek with all my heart but when he started loving his case of beer more than me, it changed. So many things changed. He was drunk more often than not and I was working long hours to avoid the chaos at home. Still, all it did was give me more work in the end. I was his wife and maid.

Lucky for me, I filed for a divorce, moved out and started living again. That might make me selfish but I don't care, because living with an alcoholic at twenty-eight years old and cleaning up his mess day in and day out got old, and you know what? I deserve better.

Work is going great. My bakery is my pot of gold. Hawkins might be a small town in Colorado but the residents sure do love my cupcakes. The firefighters across the street definitely do.

I've never been this happy, not even on my honeymoon.

Hiking by Bear Lake with my earphones on, my music keeps me going. My legs are getting tired but I'm almost at the best spot of the entire hike so I won't stop now. As my favorite song comes on, I might have added a small sway in my hips and a little bit of singing. Well, I blame Miley Cyrus for that.

While I'm walking, I don't take the time to look around me or smile at the other hikers. I mind my own business, sweat like a pig and try to breathe.

"Hey Bexley." I think I hear my name but I don't pay attention and stay on my path. "Bexley." Again, I hear my name and someone taps me on the shoulder.

I yelp, turn around, trip on a tree branch and end up sprawled on the ground.

"Jace?" I look up at him.

"Wow, are you okay? I'm sorry I didn't mean to scare you."

"What?"

He motions to remove my headphones. "I asked if you were okay and said I'm sorry I didn't mean to scare you."

I get up from the ground. "You didn't scare me, it's just that I'm focused, you know."

"Well, you should put your focus on the sky too because as you can see there's a big storm coming. I think it's started already so unless you want to finish the hike with your two feet buried in the snow, you should turn around too."

"Not yet, I'm so close to my goal."

"Bexley, I'm serious." The look of his face says it all but I've never been one to turn down a challenge.

"Turn around, Mr. Firefighter. I have maybe another five hundred metres to reach my goal so I'm going."

I put my earphones back into my ears and got back to where I was before he interrupted me.

"For fuck sake, woman!"

Running might be quicker so here goes nothing. The closer I get to my goal, the more the temperature seems to drop. My clothes are far from being warm enough. Jace was right, I have to turn around or I'm going to die or end up like Leonardo what's his name in that crazy movie and hide in a deer carcass. Was it even a deer? I don't really know, but that's beside the point. It's freaking freezing and I need to hurry back to my beat-up car.

This isn't easy, running has never been my forte and my bra isn't holding everything in place, trust me, I am putting myself in mortal danger here. A concussion and freezing to death could be my destiny. Wouldn't it be sad to die this way? I can only imagine what the local newspaper would write about me.

Bexley Dunn, 28, the local pastry shop owner has died from what appears to be a serious concussion and froze to death in the Bear Lake hiking area. There was no sign of violence on her body other than a stretched out sports bra. If there are any witnesses as to what might have occurred, please report to the police station. An autopsy will be performed on Dunn's body in hopes of gaining more information on her tragic death.

This is ridiculously insane. Out of breath, I slow down and start walking again. For a day off, this isn't relaxing. It's a full workout.

Alessia Cara's music keeps me alert but my fingers are cold as hell, so are my toes and nose.

"Oh lord, is that him?" I see Mr. Firefighter from afar. After ignoring his warning, I doubt he will turn around if I call his name. Running again, I'm trying to shorten the distance between us.

"Jace, I'm here."

Without any sign of hesitation, he turns around and runs toward me.

"Are you okay?" He asks so loud it echoes everywhere around us.

"Yes."

We run toward each other and I wonder if I should jump into his arms or not. I laugh as I run.

"What are you laughing at?" He asks quizzically as we get closer.

"Us. Are you going to save me again now, Jace?"

"Bexley… helping doesn't mean saving."

"You bought me all of my appliances when I filed for a divorce. You came running when Derek made a scene at the bakery and today, you warned me and I didn't listen."

"At this time of the year, you should always check the weather forecast before going hiking. You never know when a storm is going to roll in."

"I would if I had a TV but I still don't."

"We've got to go now before it gets worse." Jace tugs on my arm and out of the blue, he grabs my hand.

"Are we holding hands now?"

Looking up at him, I see a soft frown creasing his forehead. "I guess so. We have to hurry."

He must be well over six feet tall and I'm five feet four on a good day. "Do you realize that I have to walk twice as fast as you do just to match your stride? Your legs are much longer than mine."

"Tired already?" He doesn't slow down or let go of my hand.

"The rabbit is pushing the turtle to walk faster, I see."

"I would say I'm trying to make sure you have all ten fingers and toes tonight."

"You are so overly dramatic."

"Says the girl with the blue lips." Jace snorts, displeased by my serious lack of survival skills.

"Okay, Okay, I'm cold but I'm also out of breath."

"Oh my god, you are annoying, woman." He groans. "Can you face reality already? The mountain tops are already hiding under a thick cloud of snow. We have lost a couple of degrees since noon. You aren't dressed for the incoming weather and I don't want to be responsible for your death."

That would change the title of my article in the newspaper if I die in the arms of the favorite hunky firefighter in town. That sure would be the source of many rumors. I smile at the thought.

"You think this is funny?" Jace catches the smile on my face.

"You are being dramatic."

With that, he has enough of me. "I don't know why I'm doing this but you are getting on my nerves. I've got a way to end this." In one quick move, I find myself slung over his shoulder with my head hanging down. The view of his rear is much better than any mountain or wildlife around here. I bet it's hard with muscles too. It is very tempting to just reach out and touch.

"Are you kidding me?"

"Nope." He says and I can tell he is going a lot faster now.

Snowflakes dance their way down from the sky and I decide to let him carry me. At least I can look at the snow and beautiful view around us.

"Are you available tomorrow at five in the morning?"

"It depends, what for?"

"I need a ride to work." I laugh.

He chuckles wryly. "You annoy me too damn much. It's crazy."

"I think you like being annoyed."

"It depends."

After a while, I think he will set me down but no, he doesn't. I wave at the hikers we cross paths with and they look at us in a strange way.

That's okay, I'm relaxing.

"Okay, we're here. Be careful, I'm about to put you and your short legs down."

"You're not funny."

"I think I am."

I roll my eyes at him and wave him off. "My car is here. I guess I should say thanks for the ride."

"Wait, are you okay to drive?"

"Jace, I'm sure I can drive myself home. I'll see you around." I walk away from Jace feeling like I'm floating but stop and turn around again to see if this was real or just a dream. Snowflakes are falling on his broad shoulders and hair as he reaches his manly truck. Sighing, I get inside my rusty car with my heart feeling all kind of weird things.

Chapter 2

My car has seen better days but it's still working so I'm keeping it. There's nothing wrong with a little bit of rust. It is still a Subaru and it's amazing during the winter season.

Jace doesn't seem so sure evidently, because he has been following me from Bear Lake all the way back to Hawkins and I was following the speed limit the whole time. When I get to my apartment all defrosted by my heater, I don't expect Jace to park next to my car. In fact, he said I was annoying so many times during our trek from the woods, that doesn't sound too good.

"What does he want now?"

I get out of the car and grab my purse wondering if I should say something or just go on into my apartment.

"Bexley, do you want to grab something to eat?" Wait, What?

"Umm, I don't know. You kind of took me by surprise." To be honest, I'm speechless.

"Okay, well... it can be some other time."

With his tall legs, he eats up the distance between us and two seconds later he's standing right next to me.

"Uhh... I can do now, but can I just go up to change right quick?"

"Absolutely."

Jace King, the hottest bachelor in town has just asked me out to dinner? Me, the newly forged divorcee. We are going to be the talk of the town.

"Do you want to come up or are you going to wait here?" I ask unsure if I want to invite a man into my home. He has been inside my apartment before but it was under different circumstances.

"I can come up."

I nod and we go up the stairs. Twenty-five to be exact. Unlocking my door, I'm starting to feel nervous and it shows with my trembling fingers. "The lock gets stuck sometimes." I say to explain why I'm having trouble.

"I can take a look at it sometime this week if you want."

"I'll call the landlord. Thanks though." By some miracle, the door finally decides to spring open and I almost stumble inside.

We walk into the apartment in silence. I don't know what to say around him right now. Is he really interested in me or is this some misguided knight in shining armour syndrome?

"Are you working early tomorrow?"

"Yes, I am. Cecelia is trying to give me more freedom by doing the morning shift on the weekends but during the week, my alarm is set at 4:30am."

"That must be hard sometimes."

"It is, but if I want the bakery to have fresh bread and pastries piping hot for breakfast, I have to."

"And cupcakes. They are the best." He gives me a seductive smile that makes my heart jump.

"Yeah, you seem to be fond of them. You and the rest of the guys."

Few times a week, Jace or one of the other firefighters on shift visits the bakery to purchase a dozen cupcakes.

"It's our treat after a long day."

I blush. Business is doing well, I know but it always makes me blush when I get a compliment.

"I'm... I'm going to change and then we can go."

He smiles and nods.

I hurry to my bedroom and change. A shower would have appreciated right now. Maybe I can squeeze in a quick shower. In my underwear only I crack my bedroom door open just enough for my head to peek out.

"Jace, do you mind if I take a quick shower?"

"Not at all. In fact, I think I'll go home to shower too and I'll pick us up some takeout, that way you aren't rushed and I can shower too."

"Great. That sounds good. I'll see you in a bit."

I hear the front door ease closed as he leaves. "Jesus Christ." My back presses against my bedroom door, I feel like I'm sixteen again. Am I allowed to have a crush on Jace King? "This is so weird." How am I going to do this again? Can I fall for a man after failing the first time? I know people do this all the time but it is hard to put myself in that position. I have to give myself a second chance or else, I end up alone until I die. Hell no!

I cross the hall to my bathroom, take my underwear off and get ready for a nice warm shower.

The prickly forests that are my legs need to be mown down, not that I have any "plans" for tonight but I'm still going to be with a man, so I must be presentable.

My razor has its work cut out for it; it's a shame that I've let myself go. It's like the Amazon between my legs right now. There's a thick layer that isn't welcome at the moment.

Since Jace is coming back, I can't take my time. I want to clean the kitchen and living room before he returns as well. The day isn't going as planned. First, I had no clue about the weather, the cold front bringing snow in the mountains had me all turned around and I missed my goal. Jace happened to be on the same hiking trail I was. What a coincidence! Now, I'm about to have dinner with him and it's making me super nervous.

It shouldn't. I'm a free woman. I'm not linked to Derek anymore. I'm single, divorced, and happier. Maybe it's time I let someone take care of me. Derek failed at it for so many years. Not for my lack of trying, I did all I could to save him, or us.

All I keep asking myself is why me? There are plenty of single women in the area. I'm divorced. That means something is kind of broken with me or that I have failed right? I don't know… I just don't understand why Jace seems interested in little ol' me. It confuses me to no end.

Without wasting more time in the shower, I jump out, twist my hair into a towel and hope that I can do something simple and cute with it afterward. Naked, I run between my bathroom and my room, hoping that my favorite vintage looking skinny jeans are clean. They are. The fit of those jeans is like a second skin; they hug my backside and make it look amazeballs. Of course, I go with lace when I pick my underwear. I don't plan on showing them off but I do feel sexy wearing them and I need that little boost of confidence right now. It's all about assuming who I am. Since I left my ex, I have been taking better care of myself. Feeling pretty on the inside and outside has been making a huge difference on my mindset.

Underwear and jeans on, I dry my hair wondering what top I'm going to wear. I love my hair but it's so damn thick that it takes an eternity to dry. Thick blonde hair, my mom used to say I had Hollywood hair because my mane would make all the celebrities jealous. Done with the drying, I prep my face with my lotion to smooth the dry skin and the tinge of windburn I got on my cheeks during my hike. Mascara to add more length to my curvy eyelashes, a small amount of strawberry pink blush on my cheeks and a layer or two of kiss me gloss. Perfect!

I don't know what top to wear, but with the bombastic jeans and lingerie, I think my top needs to be neutral. A plain white tee and a baby blue cardigan. No, not the cardigan. I turn on the heat to add a few degrees and start cleaning the kitchen and living room. Do I even have something to drink? I ran out of wine last night. Damnit. I have, milk, rum and Coke, that's all. The last two will have to do.

What seems like just a minute later, the sound of a knock on my door tells me that Jace is back.

I run to the door, flip my hair to the side and open the door.

There he is, beautiful Jace and piles of takeout food. His dark hair is freshly styled giving him a clean and decadently sexy look. Let's just say that I have never seen him like this. He's stunning. His pale green eyes are locked on mine. Who is this man? I break the eye contact because I'm not ready to deal with this.

"Wow, are you really that hungry?" I ask taking the boxes from his hands to give him room to take off his boots and coat.

"Well, I didn't know what to get and the weather is going to get worse apparently so I figured at least, you'll have dinner ready tomorrow night and wouldn't have to go out into the storm." He follows me to the kitchen, I know because I can feel the heat emanating from his body behind me.

"Worse? This morning, we were surrounded by green and now, everything is covered in a thick blanket of white fluff. How much worse will it get?" I place the food on the table.

"We're in Colorado, so who knows?" He laughs. "They said it could be over a foot of snow by sunrise and possibly two feet by tomorrow night."

That sure will make my day interesting. "I'll need to buy winter boots and snow pants to get to work tomorrow."

"I think the city will be mostly shut down."

"Maybe but trust me, people are still going to want their key lime pies, fresh breads or cupcakes."

"Yeah, those things are hard to live without." He smirks. "Are you hungry now?" His raspy voice was so damn sexy.

I will eat anything if he keeps talking to me like this.

"I... uhh... I am." I blush. "What are we eating?"

"There's a Napolitano pizza, salad, lasagna and tortellini in a spicy tomato sauce. Oh, and garlic bread."

We sit at the table facing each other. It's as if there was a bonfire sparking to life under the table. His voice, the close proximity of us being alone, it makes me want things I've never thought I would again. I'm curious to know more about him and to find out more about his motives. I mean, he has been there for me more than once. This is our first official dinner date though.

I watch him as he opens up the bags of food. My eyes carefully taking stock of his face, eyes, lips, nose, even his hair.

When I was married to Derek, I never fantasized about another man. Here I am now, divorced and lusting for the firefighter I've gotten to know over the years as he came to the bakery every few days.

"Are you okay? Your cheeks, well your whole face has turned red." He chuckles quietly.

"I'm burning up. I mean, I tried to clean up before you got here. It was a real workout, trust me. Let's eat now, pizza?"

He nods and opens the box to give me a slice.

"There you go." Jace smiles as he removes a couple of pieces for himself and sets them down on his plate.

"It's quite the coincidence that we happened to be at the same hiking spot today."

"It isn't really a coincidence. Three days ago, when I was at the bakery and asked what you had planned for your weekend, you mentioned it."

"And so you came to find me?" I ask chuckling.

"It didn't happen exactly like that, but I watched the weather forecast this morning and I was pretty surprised to see that they were expecting snow tonight. I drove by your place and your car wasn't there. I figured you had decided to go regardless."

"I had no clue about the weather." Next time, I'll make sure I check.

"I decided to skip the gym and go to Bear Lake." He shrugs as if it made him uncomfortable to admit he had been looking out for me.

"Next time, I'll be more careful when you warn me not to do something."

A quick blink followed by a quirky smile. "It's okay."

The pizza smells so good, I devour it. "That's amazing." I say about the pizza. In all the years I have been in Hawkins, I've never had it before.

"You're amazing." He says, meeting my gaze above the pizza box.

I straighten up in my chair wanting him the repeat what he has just said, but I'm pretty sure I heard him right.

"Amazing, huh?" I ask not meeting his eyes.

I hear a soft chuckle. "Yeah. That's what I said. Ever since I moved into this town, I've noticed you." He moved into this town, just few months after I did. He's been paying attention that long?

"Why is that?"

"First, I thought you were beautiful but the more I got to know you the more I wanted to be around you."

"That's a lot to take in." I don't know if I'm hungry anymore so I set the piece of pizza I was holding on my plate. "So now that I'm divorced, you decided to try and get closer to me? Is that your plan?" I'm still trying to figure him out.

His mouth full, he shakes his head. "No… it's not really the plan. I thought I was in love once and it didn't work out. I never got into a serious relationship afterward. Work became my main focus and that was great for years, but I would like to get to know you more on a personal level, maybe even become friends."

I like his answer. He has me curious now.

"I work most of the time. My life is pretty boring. I don't believe I would bring much excitement to yours." The words are out of my mouth before I can stop them. It isn't what I meant to say at all. I sigh.

I keep picking around at the slice on my plate. We are basically staring at each other while eating. It's weird but I don't know, I feel like we need to get through this awkward phase.

"I'm sorry I don't have any dessert." I'm the baker and I don't even have a cake at home for dessert, how is that even possible?

"That's fine. I think I had enough anyway." He rubs his flat belly. "We should do this more often."

"I think I have an idea but it requires a small walk outside. Are you ready to face the storm?" I can't hide the excitement. It's something I have never done before.

He frowns but I can see that he's going to say yes. "Yeah okay. Let's go."

My winter boots are a must and I'm thankful I found them right away. I had no idea where I had put them after moving here. To be honest, I was convinced I had left them at the house. It's one thing I won't have to buy again. That's always a good thing.

"You should wear a scarf and hat too. It isn't pretty out there."

"What about you?" I grab my black beanie and slide it over his hair. "Sorry for messing up your hair."

"So that's how it's going to be then?" He said with a twinkle in his eye.

He grabs my Avalanche beanie from my favorite hockey team and slides it over my hair.

I laugh. "I think we're all set now."

Locking the door behind us, he waits for me down the stairs. When we step outside, it's like a slap in the face. "Oh geez, it's cold."

"I told you." Jace says holding my hand firmly.

My nipples poke out even though I have my winter jacket on. No winter attire can prepare me for this polar vortex nonsense. This is real winter, no doubt about it.

"This way." I say with my teeth chattering.

"Are you taking me to the bakery?" He asks as if he didn't already know.

I don't want to say yes but can't say no either. "Maybe."

It's obvious that I'm taking him to the bakery because everything else is closed right now. It's getting late. We already have snow up to our calves. I can only imagine how it'll be in the morning.

When we get to the bakery, he takes the keys from my hand and unlocks the door. I love a gentleman.

"Let's keep the front light turned off. I don't want people to think I'm open."

"You want to keep me all to yourself, huh?"

That right there makes me forget how cold I am. The conflagration is back and I don't know how to control it.

"Jace, do you always talk to women like this?" I ask going toward the back of the store.

"Bexley, have you seen me with any women around town before? I bet the answer is no."

When I think about it... no, I have never seen him with a woman.

"Don't get me wrong, I love being with a woman as long as it's the right one."

Still burning... temperature rising.

"What are you saying?" I think Jace wants me. It can't get any clearer than that.

"If I wasn't clear enough earlier, I'll try to shed some light on the subject. I want you. I want to be the man in your life."

"Jace... I... I just got divorced a month ago. It might be too soon." It's clear that my body reacts to him whenever he is near me, or whenever he sweet-talks me. The physical attraction is so strong that my inner self is already kissing him, devouring him. He is like a fine pastry. Pure decadent perfection. Jace is probably the only man that deserves the award of being compared to better than sex cake. I can't think about that now, it's too much all at once. I mentally facepalm myself. This is crazy and I'm an idiot. My body is reacting to him like a cat to catnip. Yes, it's that bad.

"Every time, I walk into the bakery, you come alive. Your smile is different when it's directed at me. Don't think that I'm that self-confident, the guys told me at the station." He blushes.

"It's true. I mean, it's impossible to stay unfazed by you. You are hot, sweet and so much more."

We're in the kitchen with just the security light on. The darkness envelopes us like a velvet curtain.

"I want to kiss you so bad."

Ja...Jace is sweet talking me again with that super sexy and hoarse voice. God! Fire alert, FIRE ALERT. Four alarm blaze has just ignited.

"Jace..."

I forget who I am and what I've been through. The divorce, Derek who was supposed to be the love of my life. In the here and now Jace King is standing right before me. He has been thing I look forward to the most ever since he started coming here for cupcakes. The few minutes we spent together exchanging pleasantries were always a tonic for my mood. I'll never forget that one day when I signed the divorce papers and I broke down in the middle of the bakery. The arms that supported me were his, the chest I leaned my head against was his and the cologne I hoped to smell again was... his. Maybe all this time, without admitting it to myself, my heart was already slowly falling for him.

"Why don't you?" I whisper.

"Bexley." Both of his hands came up to my cheeks. The cold coming from his hands seemed to calm the fire spreading at lightning speed throughout my body.

When his lips touch mine, it shocks me. The best way to describe the feeling would be, drinking a two hundred dollar bottle of priceless wine after drinking only box wine from the market all my life. Jace is one of those one in a million, maybe a little sweet at first but he leaves my mouth wanting a whole lot more type of guys. The simple way his lips seem to mix with mine, or how we move seamlessly together without any awkward moments, like we've been doing this all of our lives. It's flowing like the blood burning in my veins.

"Don't stop." I blow out a quick breath. My hands grab his winter jacket and I make damn sure he isn't moving.

"Bex." Jace moves his lips against mine once more. "We have all the time in the world." Maybe we do. Right now, I don't see the point of stopping the best kiss I ever had.

"You don't understand." I can't wrap my head around what is happening right now. It's surreal but a tiny part of me knew this would happen tonight.

He smiles, not that I see it per say, but I feel it on my lips. "Trust me, I do." Rubbing his lips against mine again, I take the opportunity to kiss him. He shifts his body and wraps his arms around me. I melt against him as our lips are lost in what seems to be way too intense of action for the bakery. The fire has reached my lips and has reached his. Sucking gently on my lips, I feel his arms holding me tighter in his embrace. The weight of my body is resting on him, I've lost control of my emotions and lost track of time, I'm focused entirely on that moment we're spending together.

Jace moans against my lips. The soft caress of his thumbs on my cheeks calm the fire and he lets go of my mouth.

"I promise I'll make you the happiest woman in the world." His voice does nothing to cool down my desire for him.

"You've already done a lot to make me happy over the past few weeks." The appliances he found for me, the numerous visits to the bakery and today. "You saved me today, you know?"

"You would have made it home, you're a fighter but I'm glad I was able to be there for you." He smirks. "So what's for dessert Chef Dunn?"

"Hmm… I can get you a cupcake or maybe a piece of cherry pie. You are free to take whatever you want."

"Can I have you?" Then he starts laughing as the blush stains my cheeks. "Can I have a vanilla cupcake with your dark chocolate icing?"

He will have me when the time is right. For now though, I'll give him as many cupcakes as he desires.

"Alright…" I unzip my jacket, wash my hands and get him a cake from earlier today out of the refrigerator.

When he walks out the door tonight, I hope this won't be over. If I let him into my life, and my heart, it has to mean something.

Midnight Kiss

Chapter 3

Between the two of us, we have eaten five cupcakes in the past hour. I've even let Jace put the icing on one for me. He picked a chocolate cake and milk chocolate icing. He put twice the amount of icing on the top of the cupcake but that's okay. It was a sweet moment between us.

"I think I'll have to let you get some sleep pretty soon. You'll have to wake up in a couple of hours to open the shop."

"I know."

"Come on, I'll walk you home." He offers me his hand.

"Can we go for a small walk first? The first snowfall of the year, and with it being only a week before Christmas. I'm feeling festive."

"A small walk sounds good after all the cupcakes I had."

I laugh. Three cupcakes is enough to mess up a diet plan or whatever he's doing to stay in shape. Firefighters need to be strong and healthy, right? I mean, I might have felt his body against mine once or twice, he's muscular and perfect in every way. So I doubt three cupcakes will kill him.

We get our winter attire back on. He's still wearing my black beanie which I think is adorable.

"Ready?" He asks gallantly holding out his arm for me to take.

"Yes, sir."

I close the bakery knowing I'll have to be back in less than five hours. It's okay though because I'm having a really good time and sometimes living in the moment is all I should care about.

We once again brave the storm. "Holy crap, this is why I should move to the south." There is at least one more inch of snow on the ground. This is insane.

"Have you always lived in Colorado?" I can tell I make him curious.

"I have moved so many times in my life. It's the first time I have lived in a city more than five years. I think Hawkins is where I belong, even if I have an ex-husband I would rather never see again."

"That bad, huh?" We start walking toward the wishing well and it's just a few minutes short of midnight in the middle of downtown.

"Well, let's just say I wish I hadn't married him so young."

"I was married once too. It didn't even last a year. We were only together for a couple of months when I thought we were meant to spend our lives together. We moved here before getting married because that's what she wanted and when we split, she left and I pretty much never heard from her again until she needed me to sign the divorce papers. She was wild and untamed. She wanted to see the world and be able to travel at the drop of a hat, and I wanted a career and stability, and to lay down some roots and I couldn't follow her traipsing around the globe. It taught me a lesson."

"Yeah, it taught me a lesson too. How to survive with an alcoholic husband. I thought I was handling everything until he got busted with a DUI. That was a slap in the face." For the second time tonight unless I lost track, Jace holds my hand. There's so much meaning behind the simple gesture. It calms me and I think he knows it.

"Enough about our past. You are getting all riled up." He whispers in my ear. The husk of his tempting voice is so close to my ear that goosebumps spring all over my body.

"I'm sorry, I don't want to ruin our night."

"It's far from ruined, I think it's perfect."

"It would be perfect if my eyelashes weren't transformed into Popsicles." I laugh.

"You are beautiful." He says looking at me like I am some kind of precious cupcake.

"You aren't so bad yourself." I wish I could have said something better. Jace is gorgeous and we all know it. "I've always thought you are a handsome man."

He starts laughing. "That wasn't so hard, was it?"

"You know you are hot. You are the hottest bachelor in Hawkins."

"Hawkins is a small town, I'm not fighting too hard for my throne but I'll take it as a compliment." He smiles, clearly embarrassed.

We get to the wishing well and we both bend down to look inside. Apart from all the snow that has drifted down, there's nothing to see. I try to see if I feel any magic or a strange feeling whatsoever but I don't. It's quiet and peaceful. At this time of night, everybody is home and the storm makes everything seem even more serene.

"Do you believe what they say about it? One of my clients told me we are allowed one wish." I ask.

"I've never heard about it or ever wished for anything." He runs his strong hand through his hair and stuffs the beanie back on his head, he seems like he is completely baffled about the well and the legend behind it.

"Shall we?" I ask Jace. For some reason, the air feels supercharged like change is in the wind, it makes me a little nervous.

"You want to use your one and only wish today?" He makes a cute face that I can't help but fall for.

"I do. Maybe we are allowed more than one wish too. Who knows?" I don't see rules or proof anywhere. Everything is possible.

"Okay, let's do this."

It's snowing but somehow, we can still see the full moon in between all the clouds. The setting is perfect, everything is beautiful. I feel pretty with that man next to me. It's midnight, we need to do this and head back home.

In my mind, I say my wish loud and clear. If whatever this is between Jace and I is meant to be, show me a sign. Something large that would catch my attention. It needs to be obvious because I can't make the same mistake twice. I thought Derek was meant to be my husband until death do us part and I was wrong. This time around, Jace has to be the right one or I can't do this. Getting attached to a man is a lot easier than letting him go. So if this wish thing is really working, I want a big bold red sign that I'm doing what's right. A one-night stand or friends with benefits situation isn't my cup of tea. At my age, I'm not into playing around.

"Done." He says. "I don't know what you are wishing for but with the face you are making, they'd better not disappoint."

"They better not." I repeat laughing. "I think we should head back now. I should really get to bed." As if I was going to be able to sleep after an evening like this. Jace is... wow... amazing. An amazing man.

"Yeah, it's time." He says in a low voice. Is he disappointed to go already?

We walk back with the wind blowing at our back. This time, he has his arm wrapped around my shoulder and it helps keep me warm.

I hear the cutest chuckle coming out of his mouth. "What's so funny?"

"I can't believe how my day has gone. From the minute I saw you at Bear Lake until now. I have enjoyed my day very much."

"Even when you carried me?" I should take a minute to give him a shoulder massage. Poor guy. He carried me for quite a while.

"That was my favorite part." He squeezes me closer and presses a kiss to the top of my head.

"Your shoulders might not agree in the morning?"

"Babe, I lift much heavier than you at the gym on the daily."

Blushing, I hide my face toward his chest. "Are you trying to impress me now or what?"

Even if we are just feet away from my place, he stops me in my tracks and turns me to face him. "I don't feel like I need to impress you. You seem to see me for exactly who I am."

"Pure hotness, strong arms, pretty face and good kisser, am I right?" I bat my frozen eyelashes trying to make him laugh.

"You got to see more than that. I'm trying to show you who I really am."

I touch the tip of his nose with my cold as ice fingertip. "I was teasing you. I see you how you want me to see you."

"Is that enough or do you want more?

I take a moment to answer that question. "Jace, I want the real you, no bullshit. Don't try and seduce me by being someone you aren't." We are at the same place in life, I think. We both know what we want.

"No bullshit works for me."

We agree with a kiss and we go on our separate ways. Jace walks to his truck parked by my apartment. He removes the snow that accumulated over his windshield and waves goodbye before jumping inside. I bet his hands were cold. Mine sure are. Climbing the first two steps to my door, I keep staring at Jace.

When he finally drives off, I'm shocked to discover I feel some kind of sadness. I really wanted to spend more time with him.

Chapter 4

I leave my apartment wishing I could stay home snuggled up in my warm bed. As I step outside, I notice footprints in the snow leading to and from my door. I wonder who that may be? This is the exit leading to my apartment door directly. Who could it be? It better not be Derek. So far, I have been living my life here without any interference and I don't want it to start either.

Despite the storm, the bakery is open as usual. It takes more time to get set up than normal but I have my first customer by the time it's 7. Who the hell wakes up that early during a snow storm? Apart from me that is.

"You look a little pale, Bexley. Are you feeling okay?" Marnie asks. She comes in every few days to get fresh bread and two cinnamon buns. Her husband is battling cancer and he sure loves to eat a cinnamon bun. They eat it together for breakfast.

"I'm feeling amazing, but I wasn't able to sleep much last night." I wonder why. Maybe because I kept thinking about Mr. Jace King and all the dirty things I want to do to him or with him.

"The full moon, it does that to me as well. That's why I'm late. Snow is just snow, I wouldn't be late because of that."

"There is an awful lot snow, Marnie."

"We are in Colorado, it's normal. Besides, I want a white Christmas for my grandkids."

"We all do." I smile as she removes her wool beanie. "You want the usual, Marnie?"

She nods. "Yes, please, dear."

I slice her fresh bread as usual and put two cinnamon buns in a box. "Have you started your Christmas shopping?"

"Believe it or not, I'm already done. I started early this year." She says with pride.

"That's what I say I'll do every year and somehow I never do."

"I can't deal with the Christmas shopping anymore when the mall is crowded. It makes me anxious." Marnie must be in her late sixties, I can understand the anxiety she feels shopping during the holidays.

"I will probably start shopping online."

"Yeah, well I'm too old for that."

I give her the bread and buns and she pays. The same amount counted out to the last penny, every time.

Minutes after she says goodbye, I hear the alarm from the fire station going off and they leave few short seconds later. I wonder if Jace is in there. I don't want him getting hurt. Driving through the snow might make it harder for them to do their job. The snowploughs haven't cleaned all the streets yet.

Chill out, Bex, it's his job.

For once, I chill out. I pull up my favorite playlist and listen to some of my favorite songs by Hozier while icing some cakes. The fourth coffee is starting to kick in, finally. My energy level is low but I'm starting to feel less drained. The magic of caffeine I would say.

It's almost 8 by now and I'm pretty sure my employee is about to show up. I could take that opportunity to head back to bed but I won't. Cecelia is a ray of light and pretty funny to be around.

Five minutes to 8, the bell that hangs over the door rings but she doesn't come to the back.

It must be a client, I wipe my hands on a towel and set the cake I was working on in the walk in freezer.

I walk through the flipping door and lock eyes on Derek. A drunk Derek. My heart is accelerating so much I don't know if I'm about to cry or yell at him. The footprints outside my door, it was him. He knows where I live and I bet he has been watching me.

"It has come to my attention that you have been kissing a man at midnight in the middle of town." His slurred declaration is enough to give me chills.

By saying a man, I take it he doesn't know who it is. I want Jace to stay out of it. My issues with my ex-husband can't affect him.

"What do you want Derek?" I say back controlling my emotions, I'm not afraid to fight for my own freedom.

"Who is he?" He asks with so much anger that I take a step back but he steps forward. Aggressive Derek has never happened before. Hearing about the kiss must have hurt him a lot. His hand grabs my shoulder in a way that isn't meant to be nice. Does he want me scared or hurt?

"You don't need to know who he is. We're divorced and you are also free to date who you want." It may not be the best thing to say but it's the truth. The truth sometimes sucks and might be hard to digest but it needs to be said.

"I want you." He reeks of alcohol. Memories flash through my mind of all the nights I had to look after him. Help move his drunk heavy body to the bed or over to the couch, almost every single night.

"Derek, you are drunk. You signed the divorce papers so I really don't understand what your intentions are this morning."

"When I heard that you were with someone, it hurt me so bad." His hand presses on his heart and I know he's hurting. The tears in his eyes are enough to convince me of the pain he feels. Divorce is never easy and I feel bad for him. For many years, I was his anchor, the one saving and protecting him but it wasn't a life for me. I knew I deserved more out of life than that.

"I'm sorry. I really am but there's nothing I can say now that'll make it better for you." My voice isn't as strong as it should be. I don't want to be here facing him alone. Not today, not ever.

"Take me back, I'll change. I'll be the man I was when we first got married." It breaks my heart to hear him say that. He once was an amazing husband and I'm surprised he even remembers his old self before the alcohol took over.

"Derek, please, don't do this." I'm begging him. "This isn't fair to me and you can't make promises after failing so many times in the past. Don't do this." He falls in my arms, holding me close to him.

I see Cecelia coming toward the door. She has so many layers of clothes that if it wasn't for her pink handbag, I wouldn't have recognized her. "How did you get here? Can you go back home?"

"I don't want to go home without you."

"Derek, this is my workplace. What you are doing now it isn't respectful or playing in your favor."

Cecelia walks in and realized who is hugging me.

"Good morning, Derek. You are up early or have you been up drinking all night?" She snaps.

"I had to speak to my wife here. She has been making out with some guy. I'm not okay with that." He steps back.

"And she isn't okay when you are coming to her workplace drunk off your rocker and filled with anger. What were you thinking?"

He puffs. "I'm allowed to come here. This is a public place."

I wish I could put him in his place like she just did. Flawless and to that he is speechless.

"Find a way to go home and sober up and if you still feel the need to, we'll talk later." I try to add more distance between us.

"This isn't the end." Derek points his finger at me. "The divorce means nothing to me." He walks toward the door. "Did you hear what I said? It means nothing to me. I will get you back home in no time and you won't be kissing anymore men around town."

We both watch him leave. I don't know what to think right now.

"What the fuck was that?" I say out loud.

"The better question is who the fuck did you kiss?" The glee on Cecelia's face says everything.

"A man."

"Well, good for you because as far as I know you aren't gay or bisexual. Who is he?"

"You are going to love this. Mr. Jason King himself."

"Jace? Oh my lord! You kissed Jace? You know that all the single ladies of this town are going to come after you with tar and feathers now, don't you?"

"It just happened. I can't explain it. He likes me and I think he has for a while now."

"Oh my God. That's why they keep coming to get cupcakes. They use the cupcakes as an excuse to see you. Oh, this is so much fun. It's like something straight out of one of those cheesy Netflix movies."

"No, we came here last night and we had cupcakes together. It isn't just an excuse. He really does love them."

"Wow, Wait! You came here with Jace to have cupcakes? That's so hot. The baker of the town has turned into a naughty seducer. Feed the man, girl!"

"You are crazy." I laugh.

"No, I'm not but you have changed. I think the real you is finally out of its cage. Free the bird. You are young and you are allowed to be wild."

Free the bird, really? I smile at her words.

"I think I have to agree with whatever you are saying." Cecelia lightens my mood and already I feel better. Derek's visit had the potential to mess up my day, as much as I hate to say it affects me. I have to just let it go.

The phone on the wall of the bakery starts ringing and I'm guessing someone wants to know if we are open.

I pick up the phone with a huge smile on my face. Cecelia knows how to make me happy.

"Bexley. It's Jace."

"Oh! Hi Jace. Everything okay?"

"Are you at work already?"

"I am. I saw that you guys had a call. It must be difficult getting out with all the snow."

"I'm okay, don't worry about us. I'm calling regarding your ex-husband."

"He was here a few minutes ago, completely out of his mind."

"Derek was at the bakery? What time?" *Oh no, I don't like where this is heading.*

"Like two minutes ago."

"Listen, I don't want you to panic but we found his car buried in a snowdrift on the side of the road. He probably lost control but he was nowhere around the scene. So he's probably downtown as we speak."

"I can go outside and try to find him if you want. It isn't like he could run away too far, he is far too drunk to do that."

"No, no, stay inside." I can hear the panic in his voice. "The house... it's on fire. It looks like it started in the kitchen."

"Derek's house?"

"Yes."

"Oh my god... this is terrible." It isn't even his house which makes the situation even worse. It belongs to his family. He's really ruined everything this time.

"It doesn't look too good. I'm not sure we're going to be able to save the structure." He sighs. "I'm sorry to call you concerning Derek. If you see him again, can you call 911? The police are looking for him."

"I started this, Jace. It's my fault. He's in some sort of crisis."

"Why is any of this your fault?"

"Because... because someone saw us kissing last night and told him. He's hurting."

"Damnit. I'll call you back when I have more answers. Take care, okay?" I'm pretty sure I hear a fuck echoing in the background as he ends the call.

"Yes." I start crying and place the phone on the counter nearby. My fingers are shaking and I'm not sure how I'm going to handle the situation.

"Derek is in so much trouble right now." I blurt out. Of course, I have to say more now, don't I?

"Bexley, I'm so sorry." She hugs me like a mother hugs a child, with so much love and tenderness. Cecelia is only a few years older than I am, but she is very maternal.

"Prior to coming here, he probably had an accident with his car, so he just abandoned it on the side of the road, and now the house is burning down."

"Bex, nothing about this is your fault. Derek has issues and you know that."

"I know, I know." How can this be real and not be some twisted storyline on a soap opera? "This is such bullshit. He's gone mad because he found out about me and Jace. Did he think I would stay off the market forever? It happened fast true, but trust me, I had no intention or any ideas Jace King could have a thing for me. That is still hard to believe. I mean, come on... but it's no reason to take his car out in the middle of a snowstorm drunk, and my guess is that he forgot to turn the oven off or something. Now the house is nothing but a pile of rubble. His family is going to be so mad at him now. That house had been in his family for three generations."

"Okay, sit down, take a deep breath." I do as she says but it doesn't stop the flow of tears. "I'm over and done with him but I still shared my life with him for a long time. I hope he's going to get the help he needs this time."

Police sirens echo in between the buildings on Main Street. "They are probably looking for him."

"We both know he isn't in a good place mentally but he wasn't hurt after crashing his car. I think his family will get him the help he needs or force him into treatment."

I dry the tears on my face. "They will, I'm sure they will." I groan. "I can't let him get to me like this. We're divorced and I knew one day, shit would hit the fan once I started dating again."

"I just want you to understand that your happiness with Jace shouldn't be affected by Derek's misbehavior."

I nod. "I know. I'm just mad right now."

"Be mad if you want but as soon as Jace steps back in here, you better smile and be happy."

Through the anger boiling inside of me, I still find the will to laugh. "Of course, I don't know what's going on with us right now but damn, he's such a good kisser."

"You deserve it, girl. I knew something was about to happen with one of those hot boys across the street. They keep coming in here."

"Well, first, we're the queens of cupcakes and second, come on, we're two hot babes why would they go anywhere else?"

"Hot babe for you, I'm a chubby mom."

"Shut up, you're hot. Men love women with curves."

"Oh, please! Stop with that."

"Your man thinks you are hot. I know because I see the way he's looking at you every time he comes in to drop off your lunch. The bakery about burned down last week from the heat in his gaze."

Now, her face is flushed and my work is officially done.

Cecelia is beautiful and I love having her on my team. At seventeen, she became a mom but it didn't stop her from realizing her dreams. She finished high school and she went on to get a baker diploma. She's had it rough but right now, she's indispensable to my shop. Her passion and talent are bringing different ideas which the customers love.

Both of us are laughing despite the shit my ex-husband is going through. He isn't my problem anymore and the trouble he put himself in shouldn't affect me. Right?

"What should we do today? I mean, I don't think we're going to be too busy."

"I was just thinking the same thing. I'll get a few loaves of bread in the oven and I think we could discount what we have left from yesterday and start fresh tomorrow. I doubt it'll be a busy day."

"It sounds good to me."

We got to work and now that I'm in my happy little bubble, my thoughts are back with Derek. The policemen probably have him in custody already and I hope Jace is safe doing whatever he has to do to stop the fire. It's scary for me but it's just a typical day for him.

He must be so freaking sexy in his gear. I've never seen him wearing the full suit. My thoughts of Derek's misery vanish completely when Jace shows up in my mind. It's still unbelievable.

I made out with him. ME! This is insane. Of course, I'm attracted to him but I never thought he could be attracted to me.

"You have it bad, my friend."

"Shut up."

"You are smiling as if you had just won the lottery."

"Maybe I have."

I totally won the lottery when that fine specimen of a man kissed me under the full moon. It was the best feeling I have felt in forever. He is the icing of my cupcake.

"You are so falling for him already."

"Cecelia, please stop or I'm going to be a blubbery mess if it doesn't work out. I have to keep things as grounded in reality as possible and not let my heart in too deep."

She stares at me for a moment, thoughtful. "I don't think he's going to break your heart. He has been coming here for a while, had small talks with you every chance he's got. King has been planning this for a while."

King wears his name right. King of my heart and we've only shared one dinner and few kisses. Who am I kidding now?

"I think he did too and I never noticed it until now. I'm oblivious I guess."

"You weren't ready for it, that's my guess."

I go back to my bread preparations daydreaming about Jace. Will he come over after everything is finished? Will I see his face covered in soot? That would be so sexy and manly. Hell yes.

I put the bread in the oven and join Cecelia standing by the front windows and looking at the snow falling.

"Whenever there was a snowstorm like this when I was a kid, I would go outside and cover the front lawn of our house with snow angels."

"I used to make a snowman." I add. "Angels too though sometimes."

Opening the front door of the shop, she pulls me outside laughing and at the same time, we flop down on the thick layer of snow.

"Holy crap, it's cold out here."

We laugh so much my belly hurts.

"Are you done?" She asks still moving her legs and arms in the cold fluffy snow.

"I'm freezing. My butt is going to have frostbite." I giggle and almost pee my pants. "Come on, let's get back inside and I'll make us two hot chocolates."

She is back up in no time while I can't manage to get the strength as I'm laughing too much. With her hands locked around my wrist, she pulls me back on my feet.

"It's good to be a kid sometimes."

The two firefighters left at the Hawkins Fire Department, Ladder 12 are watching us wondering what's going on.

"We're okay, don't worry." I wave at them.

"At least, they are smiling." Cecelia pushes me inside and it's so good to feel the warmth seep into my bones again. "Today is turning out a lot better than I thought."

"I should send you home to be with your daughter. It's not busy enough for both of us to have to be here."

She shrugs. "I can't say no to that, but I want my hot chocolate first."

"Duh, of course."

I get the milk warm enough and add just the right amount of cocoa and sugar and few pieces of marshmallow.

"There you go."

"Thank you, future Mrs. King."

I almost drop my cup. "Cecelia, don't say that. It's way too soon and I said I would never marry again."

"As if you could resist him if he gets down on one knee."

"Oh, please stop, we've only kissed so far. We didn't do anything more and I still have so much to learn about him."

"You are already considering it though and I call that progress." She hugs me. "I'm just giving you a hard time but seeing you this happy after only one date is amazing."

"Take a cupcake to go for your daughter."

"Nice try, don't change the subject. Why won't you admit that he makes you feel good?"

I roll my eyes. She won't let it go, she wants to hear it from me. "You surely know by now that he makes me feel a good deal of happiness. Isn't that good enough for now?"

"Yes." She nods toward the station across the street.

One of the trucks is coming back. I wonder if Jace is back now.

Cecelia grabs two cupcakes. "Put the other one on my tab."

"Just take it."

We drink our hot chocolate in silence. Well, let's say that I'm too busy focusing on what's going on over at the station to keep up an intelligent conversation.

"I bet he's going to come running over here the minute he's back."

"I hope so."

I never cared much when I saw them leave for an emergency before but now, it makes me anxious. He'd better be back in one piece soon.

Midnight Kiss

Chapter 5

It's getting late and I didn't have more than two handfuls of customers after Cecelia left. I sold a lot of my discounted cakes and pies and my fresh baked bread was gone in a matter of two hours. This time, I'm bringing home a cake and cupcakes. I haven't heard from Jace since he called earlier and that's fine. He was busy working, that much I know.

The city road crew cleared the sidewalks but snow is already accumulating again. I'm out of breath by the time I reach my apartment. Climbing the stairs with two boxes filled with desserts in more than I can handle. A lack of sleep never does me any good and my legs are starting to hurt from the hiking I did yesterday. I hadn't thought about that when I tried to prove Jace wrong.

Finally home, I place the boxes on the counter before removing my boots.

"Good idea, Bexley, now there's snow everywhere."

I clean up my mess and I'm ready to lay claim to my bed already.

The leftovers from last night are calling my name, I'm hungry and cold.

Pastas are going to be perfect if only Jace could show up here to share them with me. I asked for a sign and so far, I haven't seen one. The legend of the wishing well is probably bullshit anyway.

Whatever...

If I learned anything today that is Derek is a lost cause and I hope his family is going to save him rather than inherit him. Deep down, he's a good man but with the alcohol addiction, he got lost along the way.

The doorbell chimes, interrupting my thoughts.

I push the button on the intercom. "Who's this?"

"Flower delivery, ma'am."

"OK." I push the button to unlock the door.

Flowers? The last time I had flowers it was my wedding day.

"Good evening, Ma'am." He gives me a large bouquet of red roses and a red box.

"You deliver flowers after hours now?"

"Not usually, Ma'am but Mr. King can be quite persuasive."

"I'm sorry you had to come here with all the snow out there." I feel bad for the poor guy.

"It's my pleasure. You have a good evening now."

"Thank you and you as well."

He turns around and goes down the stairs while I lock my door again.

I remove the wrapping paper around the bouquet and place the bouquet in my largest glass because I don't have a vase. Why would I need a vase? It's not like I ever get any flowers? I say to myself remembering the vase I left behind at Derek's house.

Twenty-four red roses. It's too much but they are so pretty.

I take the red card out from the arrangement and tear the envelope to read what it says.

Bexley,

Last night was everything to me.

I hope the feeling is mutual.

I'll stop by tonight.

Jace

I read the card at least five times in a row and turn it around to see more red roses printed on the card.

Maybe that's my sign. It's red. It has to do with Jace.

Wow! Could this be it? Is the wishing well real?

Really?

I'm in shock. I open the second box and nestled inside are six strawberries dipped in milk chocolate. There's also a card on it.

Tonight, I'm bringing dessert.

"Oh my God!"

The temptation to eat one, and by one I mean all of them is strong but my mind goes in a different direction. What if I feed Jace a strawberry before kissing him? That sounds perfect. I'll wait.

Before he gets here, I'll try to shower and change into clean clothes. Nothing too fancy because I'm no princess and comfort always wins.

My phone rings and jolts me from my fantasy. Jace.

"Hello."

"Bexley. It's Jace. Are you home?"

"Jace, thank you so much for the flowers and strawberries."

"It's nothing. I missed you and guessed that you probably had a rough day so..."

"It's all better now."

His voice in my ear is the apex of my day. Amazing!

"Can you unlock the door? I'm downstairs, on my way up."

"Already?"

"Yeah, I couldn't wait to see you." The soft sound of his chuckle melts my heart.

I unlock the door and wait for him to reach the top of the stairs.

In a bright red hoodie and dark wash blue jeans, he looks handsome. Sexy as hell, too. And its RED, that's gotta be another sign, right?

"Hey, beautiful." He says and my heart sings.

"Hey, sexy." I say back and regret it right away.

"Sexy, huh? I'm not even trying." He meets me climbing the stairs two at a time.

"You don't need to try, it just comes natural to you.."

His lips crash on mine as soon as he walks in. "I'm sorry I couldn't be here sooner."

"It's okay." I know what kept him busy all day. This is work for him and it is clear that he has had his hands full with the fire.

"I'm sorry about the shit day you probably had." The compassion he shows me in this moment touches me.

"It's okay." I repeat. "You're here now. Plus, you spoiled me rotten already."

"I couldn't stop thinking about you. All day, when I should have been focusing on work, all I could think about was you."

"Sorry?" I bit my lips.

"Don't be sorry, please." He kisses me again. This time, his cold hands come up to cup my cheeks as he holds me in place.

"Are you okay? You had a long day, you must be exhausted."

He smiles. "I'm okay."

"I was about to warm up the leftovers from yesterday. Are you hungry?"

He nods and follows close behind into the kitchen. His arms come around my waist while I place the pasta in the microwave.

"Do they have him now?" I ask because I need to know.

"Yes, they do." It's all I needed to hear. "Don't worry about it. He's taken care of."

"Good." I lean back against him and relax while the food is warming up. "I just want to stay like this."

"Then, do." He holds me tighter. "Is it okay that I've missed you today?"

"Absolutely. Cecelia is pretty thrilled about us. I mean, I don't know what the future holds for us but she likes the idea."

"And, what about you?"

I take a moment to answer. "The fact that I'm beyond happy to see you here tonight says a lot about how I feel. I know you are a good man, caring, gentle and you have such a sexy voice. I bet you can seduce any woman you want with just your voice and looks. What we have now, I'm interested." Small kisses pepper my neck. "I'm interested too... Most definitely." More kisses land on my neck.

"Jace... the food is ready."

He takes the plate and places it on the table. I grab us some forks and we sit side by side at the table. We start eating from the same plate.

"You'll be pleased to note I have desserts this time. I'm prepared for your sweet tooth."

"Why? Didn't you like our impromptu visit at the bakery?"

"I did, very much. I don't think I'll ever forget that night but I would rather have privacy now and stay out of the public eye. I may have spies."

"I think we do."

I sigh. "That's the only way Derek could have found out."

"I don't regret it, even after the day I had."

A wave of joy crests over me. "Am I really worth the trouble?"

"Yes. Without a doubt." He feeds me a forkful of lasagna. "I'm here right now with you."

"I was hoping you would come over tonight." I admit with a grin tugging up my lips.

"Did you bring cupcakes?"

I start laughing even with my mouth full. I nod. "And more."

He kisses my cheek. "You're a keeper."

"So are you." So far.

Out of nowhere, Jace gets his sexy booty up and take his hoodie off. All I'm thinking is please God, tell me he has a shirt on underneath or I'm going to choke on this pasta or pass out. "It's really hot in here." At least I'm certain he is capable of doing lifesaving mouth-to-mouth breathing if necessary. Jesus Christ, I've got to steer my thoughts in a different direction before my ovaries implode.

"Oh, I'm sorry. Maybe I shouldn't dress so sexy. It would give you a break." Not a second passes before I regret saying that. That should have stayed in my head. I'm wearing the bakery shirt and black jeans, this isn't sexy. It isn't even casual.

Laughing out loud, Jace is losing a battle between his hoodie and T-shirt which doesn't seem ready to part ways.

That's it, he's going to end up shirtless in the middle of my kitchen and I'm going to have so many dirty thoughts in my head. I have to look elsewhere but I can't. My neck is locked in his direction.

"Do you need help?" I offer. Any reason to touch him is good.

"Oh fuck it." He says removing both tops at the end.

Shirtless firefighter alert! Tattoos, muscles, abs, muscles, abs, tattoos, muscles, abs...

"Bexley, are you drooling?" He lowers his eyes to my level. "You're cute, you know that?"

"Cute? I look like a grandma next to you. What are you saying, abs of steel? I don't understand how you can eat all those cupcakes and still look this way? Are you even eating them?" I ask giggling.

"I'm saying I don't want a woman with abs of steel. I want a woman who's real, soft and with curves. You are the woman I've been desiring for a long time now."

"You are in a really good shape."

"I work out a lot when I'm at the station, there's a lot of downtime when we are on call. That's all." He pulls his T-shirt from his hoodie and hides all the perfectness from my amazed eyes.

"Stay like this." Wait, what? "If you're too hot I mean."

The pink on his cheeks is turning into a rosy glow. "It's okay. I'll be all better now."

I manage to get more pasta into my mouth before my brain decides to add more stupidity to our conversation.

He sits back next to me and this time, I feed him a bite.

"Do you have any plans for after dinner?" He asks.

"No, I mean, it's not like we could go anywhere. It's like the North Pole out there."

"It is, but we can't let that stop us from having the time of our life."

"Jace." I say his name out of speechlessness.

"The bowling alley isn't far."

"Why not stay inside tonight?" More snow is coming and I prefer to stay warm for now. "I have more sweets if you want more later." The fact that I'm a baker might ruin his perfect silhouette. I might have used a different approach if I don't want to make a Homer Simpson body out of him.

"If one day I'm diabetic, it's on you." See? I think he sees right through what I'm doing.

"Jace, control and moderation is everything in life." That makes me sound like such a grown-up. It's unreal.

"What if I can't keep it when I'm around you?"

Does he mean control? Jace can't control himself when he's around me? Is that right or am I going insane?

"Oh, you are a strong man, King, I'm pretty sure you can control yourself around me." My face heats up. He affects me as well.

"You make me want to live and do crazy things."

I smile because it flatters me. "You are a firefighter, you do crazy things every day, I bet."

He shrugs. "Take the compliment. You are driving me crazy." Jace looks away for a second and then, looks back into my eyes. "Pack a bag, and bring the dessert. We're going to my place."

"What?" I feel the panic rise down in my heart. "I'm not sure I heard you right."

"Pack a bag, the weather's bad. If it gets worse, you can sleep over at my place. I have a comfortable couch or a guest room."

I nod and stay at the table as if both of my legs were paralyzed. This is major. By asking me to pack a bag, we've skipped at least 5 steps. This is living dangerously. Hello Bexley, it's the age of dangerous. I've been locked in a home taking care of an alcoholic most of my life. Now, it's time I take some risks. "O-Okay. Sure. Pack a bag. That's simple enough."

I get up from my chair and almost fall flat on my face.

"Bexley, we can stay here if you prefer. Going to my place isn't worth a panic attack."

"I'm not having a panic attack, you simply took me by surprise." I manage to shake it off and pack the damn bag. Cute pajamas and a change of clothes for tomorrow. "You do realize that I have to be at the bakery in the morning?" I say out loud from my bedroom.

Steps echo through the living room and I see Jace come down the hallway and then, lean against my bedroom doorframe smiling like he's some kind of romance novel cover model. "I think I know, Bexley and I do have an alarm clock."

"Convincing enough. My bag is packed, sir. I'm ready to go."

"Sweet. You do really need a television in here. I don't know how you can live without one. It gets pretty quiet when you live by yourself."

"Oh, don't worry about me. I have an iPad and that does the trick. I can watch movies, news, listen to music, pretty much everything."

"Oh, please." Jace grabs my bag and we both grab our jackets and boots. "I'll accept your lame excuse because you have just moved in, but you need a television."

"Okay, okay... I'll get one... someday." I giggle.

Jace takes my keys. He locks everything behind us and holds my hand all the way to his pickup. He owns a big truck and it sort of fits with his whole persona. Strong and virile, able to plough through anything. While he removes the snow from the windows and hood, I try not to create any type of expectations on what the rest of the night will be like. Already, I had no intention of going out and here I am, out.

Go with the flow. Take it easy and I know, Jace isn't the type of man to force anything on me. If THAT was his intention, I think he would have tried before. Right?

Jace joins me in the car. The poor man looks cold as hell. His cheeks are red but not from blushing. It's freezing outside. Starting up the engine, he turns the heat to the max and starts driving away.

"It just occurred to me, I have no clue where you live."

"You have probably driven past my house thousands of times already. You just didn't know it's mine."

"Now, I'm curious." I mean, it could be any house in town. Right now, it's impossible for me to guess which one it is.

"You'll see soon enough. It isn't too far."

Country music is playing softly in the background. I'm not really fond of country music but since it isn't my car, I'm dealing with it. Maybe Jace is the biggest country music fan ever. There's so much I still need to know about him.

Two minutes later, after driving in the worst conditions possible, Jace makes a turn into a driveway.

Oh! That house. I nod. "I've noticed that house before only because you have the biggest BBQs in the summer and there are always cars parked everywhere."

"That's it. I like having people over when the weather allows it." This isn't a typical get together, it's a massive BBQ. Kids playing around the houses or in the pool. His whole yard is filled to capacity. Cecelia went to one last summer with her brother, that's how I know all the details.

"Even when the weather doesn't allow it, you find a way to invite someone over."

He leans his head to the side. "You are right." He digs behind my seat and grabs my bag. "No expectations whatsoever. It's basically just like a sleepover. Like kids do."

I start laughing at his attempt to make me feel comfortable. "And here I was hoping to get another kiss. Now, that's a bummer."

"Babe, I want to steal one right now."

Jace kisses the corner of my mouth and pulls away enough to catch my gaze. When he sees the agreement or lust in mine, he caresses my cheek with his icy fingers.

"You're beautiful, Bexley."

Again, he brushes his lips against mine, tempting me. I breathe harshly growing impatient for that kiss. As our lips brush, he pulls me closer to him. I exhale and close my eyes before breathing again. Oh God! He runs his tongue over my lips and again, it seems like he's only teasing me.

I make the first move and kiss him. Jace kisses me back, trust me on that. He's devouring me like he devoured the cupcakes earlier. Our tongues are dancing, touching in a way I've never experienced before. . It's sexy, hot...but I'm still not crossing that line.

Every fiber of me wants it. If he kisses this way, I can only imagine how he'll manage the act.

I grab his coat and whimper into his mouth.

He pulls back. "Jesus, woman. You are taking my breath away. Come on, let's go inside before this happens again."

Well, chalk one up for me, I've made Jace King completely dumbfounded.

Chapter 6

As we walk into his home music was playing in the background. A powerful male voice with an air of melancholy is leading the melody.

"Do you always leave music playing in your house or do you live with someone?" I ask removing my boots.

"I always leave it on. The house doesn't feel too lonely when I have music playing."

I look around once I hand my winter coat over to Jace. The space is open and inviting. "I think your living room and kitchen are the size of my whole apartment."

"I like your apartment, it's warm and cozy. You made it feel like home while I haven't done that yet around here."

"What are you saying? You have a beautiful home!"

"I still feel like a stranger wandering the halls most days."

He walks toward me and I feel the warmth in me spreading again.

"You have been living here for a while though." I try to distract myself with a conversation.

"Yes, I have." He adds wrapping his arms around me. "The yard is perfect for large BBQs with my friends, so is the house for Thanksgiving and Christmas but I don't have the *home* feeling."

"It's something you have to build. Paint and decoration can do wonders."

"I might need your help. A woman's touch." He says kissing my neck, my jaw and finally my lips.

Can the passion between us get any hotter?

The kisses intensify as we go from standing in the entryway to the couch.

He sits first and ends up lying down with ME on top. Oh my God. This can go any direction right now.

Could I?

I mean, could I sleep with him? Now? Tonight?

Maybe.

The thought scares me a little.

"Bexley, everything okay? Do you want to slow down?"

"No, it's fine. It's just that I was starting to wonder if I could sleep. No, ugh I mean — have sex with you tonight?" I pull away, and sit at the opposite side. "Sorry for ruining the moment."

"You aren't ruining anything. If you aren't ready, I won't be the asshole forcing you. We have all the time in the world."

"You have always been so sweet and gentle with me from the start."

I've got nothing wrong to say about Jace. He's more than I ever imagined.

"Do you want to watch a movie, on a TV?"

"Oh geez, you have a TV. How weird is that?" I make fun of him. "No horror movies, please."

"Are you going to sit there all night or are you going to come closer? I won't bite you."

"I know you won't." I scoot closer with a fake ass smile on my face. It's not that he did something wrong but somehow I think I may not be ready for this. The first guy I meet that shows interest in me after Derek and I'm going through a block. It's a battle between my heart and my head. I know my heart wants every inch of him and more. My head is tempted, and I do mean very tempted but it doesn't give in.

Not because of Derek. I'm so done with him.

So then why?

Sex with Jace is a guaranteed good time. He kisses like a God. Imagine for a second just how good sex could be or will be with him?

"Are you okay? You seem like you're somewhere else."

"I like being with you, Jace. It's like you are the ray of sunshine of my days, the light in my darkness. You make everything better like a body cream on dry skin. I mean it may not be the best example but you soothe me. But why does it scare me so much with you when you're such a good kisser?"

"Hmm, I don't know, Bexley. I think you should answer that question yourself. If you aren't into it now, it's okay. I'm not forcing you. Yes, it got pretty heated a few minutes ago but that doesn't mean I'm going to run away if we don't take the next step tonight." He explains softly. "I couldn't anyway. I'm way too attracted to you. You are driving me insane."

I take the decorative pillow next to me and hide my face into it. "Stop, it's not helping."

"Oh, please." Jace shakes his head laughing and pulls me closer to his side before wrapping an arm around me. "So, you said no horror movies right?"

"Christmas is around the corner, what about a nice Christmas movie?"

"Hmm like what? Home Alone?"

"No, a romantic one. They have tons on Netflix."

Jace doesn't seem entirely enthused about my idea. "Really? Aren't those movies super predictable, no action whatsoever?"

"Okay, Mr. Firefighter, put on whatever you want and it'll be fine with me as long as it isn't horror." I say cuddling up next to him. I love the feeling of being close to him.

I might just not be ready for more. Can I not be ready at my age? I guess so.

"Okay." His answer is short and unlike him. After scrolling through the list for a while, he ends up choosing *The Boy Next Door.* I have seen this movie so many times. Let's say I was fond of the actor.

The movie begins and Jace is still quiet. Maybe he doesn't like being called Mr. Firefighter. I snuggle closer and put my legs over his. A subtle corner smile appears on his mouth.

"You are my teddy bear." I say and I'm surprised I've even said that. With Jace I always feel safe and comfortable. Isn't it what teddy bears are for?

"Am I?"

I nod. "Yes. I'm sorry for being complicated."

"Don't worry about it. It has been a very long day and it's only the second time that we've hung out." He kisses my forehead and tucks me into his side and focuses back on the movie.

While he watches the movie, I watch him. The little lines at the corner of his eyes when he laughs or how he bites his lips when the actors make out and how his hand drops down to caress me at the very same time. It gives me chills.

"Are you cold? Hold on, I'll get a blanket." Without getting up from the couch, he stretches his arm out to a wicker basket and grabs a fleece camouflage blanket. "Don't ask about the camo. It was for hunting. I went last year and hated it."

"It's soft."

"That's why I kept it." He adds wrapping me up like a burrito. "Better?"

I nod. "Yes."

Once I'm warming up in the blanket, he wraps his arms around me.

"You smell so good, I could stay like this forever." He says with that low and sexy voice.

"After a while, the perfume will wear off and you'll find that very unattractive."

"Woman, I've been hooked on you forever. Trust me that it won't matter." I love when he says things like that to me. It's different than being treated as a maid.

"Hooked on me forever." I repeat, turning my head and kissing his shoulder. "That's kind of flattering."

"It should be. I waited in the wings long enough and I'm pretty sure Derek knew the entire time."

"What makes you think that he knew?" Now, he has me curious. What a way to pique my curiosity.

He puts the movie on pause.

"Remember, maybe, three months ago, at Cassie's Steakhouse when…"

"When the waiter spilled Derek's beer on me? How could I forget?"

Jace laughs. "I felt so bad for you. I rushed to your table with napkins and asked if you were okay before Derek had a chance to. We laughed together but Derek was furious."

"I know. Wasting a beer is tragic." I sigh. "That was actually supposed to be a romantic dinner for his birthday. It sure didn't turn out that way."

"You were gorgeous. I had never seen you like that. Not at the bakery or when I ran into you in town somewhere running errands."

"Thank you… I don't dress up very often." I yawn.

He puts the movie back on and I snuggle back into him.

"What are you doing for Christmas? Do you have family plans?"

I shake my head. "No, it's the biggest, busiest time of the year at the bakery, I stay in town and work my ass off to make sure everything is delivered on the 24th or the morning of the 25th."

"You already work long hours, you will be exhausted."

He is right about that. I'm already exhausted and it isn't Christmas yet so I can only imagine how I will be when the time comes.

"I know but that's how it goes. Cecelia helps out a lot and she's someone I trust too. I normally celebrate Christmas around the 28th. I fly home and stay the night, or they fly here and spend Christmas with Derek and me whenever I get off work. We always make it work."

"I want to spend Christmas with you. I know it doesn't give you much time but I would love if we could spend part of the day together."

My heart speeds up. "Really? You want to be with me?"

"Of course, silly. We could try and do something special even if you have to work." He kisses my head.

I nod against his arm. "I want a Christmas tree. I left everything behind when I packed my things. At the time, it didn't cross my mind and now it's probably burnt to a crisp." I haven't called my parents and they haven't called either. Nothing is planned and we are just a few days away from Christmas. It's unlike me, but I've had a lot on my mind since I moved out of Derek's.

"Don't worry about it. I'll help you with that."

If I need a man in my life, it's him. "Thank you."

"Are you comfortable?"

"Of course I am. You are warm and I love cuddling with you. Plus, you smell amazing."

I try to push myself higher to reach his lips. Once he realizes what I'm doing, he helps me up and our lips collide.

"I don't know what I've done to deserve you." There is so much truth behind those words. Everything he is doing for me, I don't understand.

"I was just thinking the same thing." His lips find mine again. He keeps it short but the intensity gets high fast.

"I don't think we should kiss anymore tonight. It gets more dangerous every time." He chuckles.

"Right. No more kissing." I giggle.

In silence, we put our focus back on the movie and slowly, the TV gets blurrier by the second. I try to force my eyes to stay open but soon I lose the battle and my eyes drift closed.

"Bexley, babe, you have to wake up. The alarm on your phone has been ringing for a little while."

"Oh no!" I jump up from wherever I am but as the view around me settles, I remember I'm not home and instead, I'm in Jace's bedroom. Dizzy, I sit back on the bed. Today is going to be rough.

"What time is it?"

"5:30."

"Ugh. Can I shower before I go?"

"Why don't you stay with me a little longer?"

The temptation to say in bed is much greater than I want but the small amount of will still in me makes me get up and stretch. I notice that his side of the bed is still untouched. Where did he spend the night?

"I sleep on top of the covers. Sleeping on the couch might have been the right thing to do but I couldn't. That's the best I could do."

I nod shyly. The fact that he couldn't bring himself to sleep on the couch makes me blush. "Where's the bathroom?" I ask.

He follows me out of the bed, wraps his arms around my waist and guides me toward the bathroom. "Towels, shampoo and soap are all in there, I think you are all set." His lips find my neck. "You're cute in the morning, even with puffy eyes."

"Oh, please, Jace. I look like a mess."

"My mess."

My mess? Oh, are we to that stage?

"Your mess?"

"Yeah. My mess." He grins. "My girl. You."

Hearing him say those words gave me teary eyes. Jace wants me as his, for real! The idea of him playing never crossed my mind but he really does want me.

"Are you my mess too?"

"Only if you want me to be?"

He removes the small teardrop from the corner of my eyes.

"You're my mess too." I pull him by the elastic band of his boxer briefs. Why is he so sexy in morning? While I'm still fully dressed in my clothes from yesterday, he's only wearing red boxer briefs. I know, red. The universe keeps sending me sign. It's okay now, I get it. It's him. Jace is a keeper.

It might be my brain still being groggy but I pull my top over my head and my pants down.

"Do you need to shower too?" I ask him wondering where this newfound sense of courage is coming from.

"Bex... are you sure?" He lifts my chin up with the tip of his index finger.

"Don't make me doubt myself, Jace."

"Alright." He gets the water running and we move under the warm water half-naked.

"I respect your boundaries, last night..."

"I know."

I want more of him. We spent our first night together and I was too exhausted to enjoy it. He moved me into his bedroom without me even noticing.

I reach the clasp behind my back, ready to remove my bra and reveal myself to him. My heart is pounding as if I had never done this before. It's hard to believe that I am doing this but I only have one life to live and Jace seems to want to be part of it.

I might have gotten my wish in the end.

"I don't know what to…"

"Jace, don't stop me. It's taking everything in me to do it, to take the next step. I want to, I swear."

My hands are replaced by his and as softly as I could ever ask for, he removes my bra, allowing it to slide off my arms. I expected him to touch or look but he didn't. Instead he takes me in his arms and moves us under the water. His lips collide with mine, his hands are everywhere around me, holding as much as caressing me. My skin comes alive so does every part of my body.

We're not even having sex yet and I feel like he's going to make me reach for the stars and fall from the clouds in the most beautiful way.

Entwined in his hair, my fingers hold on to him for dear life. I suck on his lips as if they were lollipops. My breathing is loud and my body seems to be high on him. I melt against him allowing the heat from his body to seep into mine.

"We're going to have to slow down now, baby."

I pull away from him for a moment. Sucking in air, my body feels like I've just run a marathon. What's going on with me? Am I on the verge of going insane?

"That… what have you done to me? I feel like I've hit puberty again and I'm discovering the joys of making out."

"That's not funny, Bexley, you are… the most… I can't even put it into words."

"You're at loss for words?"

"Yeah." He adjusts his groin.

"Oh!" Holy shit. "Jace."

I have to think fast. I mean... maybe we should go for it and then, we'll see what we are about. Make it or break it.

Not that I have any doubt in my mind about him.

But. You never know.

Without wasting more time, I push my wet panties down my thighs and I watch his face as he gulps.

"O-okay." He whispers with water running down his face in rivulets. Such a nice sight to start the day.

"Yes." I step closer to him and he doesn't move I slide my fingers underneath the waistband of his underwear. Still, he makes no attempt to help or stop me so I push them down as I did with mine. Our eyes locked together, I see a sheen of lust or desire covering his. He wants me, maybe even more than I do. He has been waiting for me for a lot longer.

"Not here." He says when his drenched boxer briefs hit the shower floor.

"Why not?"

"Come on, if we're going to do this, you deserve better than a quick romp in the shower."

He pulls my hand not leaving me a choice but to follow him out. Once we are by the bed, he cups my face with his two hands and slowly pushes me down on the mattress. The weight of his full naked body on mine is turning the burner back on. He's warm, soft and more than I could have imagined.

"I don't have any condoms." He says as he stretches over to his nightstand and rummages through the top drawer.

"Oh... I'm on the pill and I haven't been sleeping around, as you probably know."

"Okay... okay... so we're good?"

I nod and he starts kissing me right away.

If he doesn't have any condoms, it shows that he didn't have intentions of sleeping with me last night or he would have been ready. Right? I mean, a man who's only after sex would think about those kinds of things... I think.

Enough about the condom conspiracy, I have this handsome man kissing me and making my body sing Amazing Grace. This can't get any better.

As the epic make out session keeps on going, our bodies slowly fall into a natural rhythm and it is as natural as icing cupcakes.

My hand drifts from his strong shoulders to his hard as a rock sculpted backside. This is perfection. I can't help but compare him to Derek even if I shouldn't but the difference is too important.

It's the same as cruising in a tank then driving a Rolls Royce.

"Jace." I say in a low voice.

"Are you okay?" He asks with that sexy voice.

"Okay isn't right. It's amazing. You are amazing."

This moment we are sharing is special in every sense. I've never been treated so exquisitely by a man. The way he kisses or touches me is so delicate and respectful, yet I also feel his desire and virility behind every move he makes.

The sensation down there is building into a perfect O. My toes curl, my fingers are gripping the sheets or Jace's hair, anything I can hang onto at this point.

The rhythm of ours speeds up, getting us both to that point. The crescendo we are both striving for.

"Jesus, Bexley, if you don't stop gripping me like that I won't."

Of course, the naughty little devil in me tightens the grip.

Jace groans into my neck. "You're killing me."

"I think we are pretty amazing if you ask me."

I meet him thrust for thrust. By the sound of his breathing or the sweat covering his pretty face, I know he's close to the edge.

It keeps building and getting bigger or heavier in my belly. It is a foreign feeling but I don't mind getting better acquainted with it. Jace groans again and somehow throws my name in there.

His lips continue to devour mine and BOOM... the big O spread from down my sex to every nerve cell in my body like an atom bomb would do, a shockwave the likes of which I've never experienced. I have no clue what's even happening after. I think I'm losing it. My body is melting against Jace. His beating heart becomes my primary focus as my body floats through heaven on earth.

Breathe. I feel so good in his arms. It's the best feeling in the world.

"Bex, you have to get up now or you'll be mad that I've let you sleep in."

"What time is it?"

"It's 8 am. I called Cecelia and she's fine taking care of things until you make it in."

"Jace King, I've never been late. What are you doing to me?"

"Well, I think I'm doing good things to you. You seemed pretty pleased actually."

I jump out of his bed naked and to the shower I really need to take now.

At that moment, it hits me. We didn't use protection. I'm the first to hate condoms but that wasn't a smart move. My cousin got pregnant while she was on the pill. Then I start counting to know if I'm in the dangerous days of my cycle but

I'm not. I shouldn't worry about it. I mean, the statistics are good with the pills, right? I breathe in and exhale.

It'll be okay.

Right?

Chapter 7

It's four in the afternoon and I haven't heard from Jace since he dropped me off here this morning. I mean it's okay but I thought he would come by at some point during the day.

"I think the mix is okay. You have been stirring for the last ten minutes now."

"I thought the dough was too thick." I sigh. "I'm lying, I was thinking about Jace."

"How is it going with him?"

I know she is dying to know about us and the reason why I was late this morning.

"I spent the night with him at his place last night but trust me it wasn't as romantic as it sounds. We made out, yes, but I passed out while we were watching a movie and only woke up this morning. Then, we, umm..." The blush that rose to my cheeks burned as hot as a four-alarm blaze as images from this morning flash back into my mind. Yes, it was that amazing. I didn't make it to the bakery until almost 10 am because Jace couldn't keep his hands off me as I tried to get ready. Not that I'm complaining. "That is the only good reason that would make you come in late. It has never happened before."

"Well, I could see it happening again." I confess.

"So, it's getting serious already?"

"I don't know. Maybe. It's hard to tell for sure but I'm trying not to get too attached, you know?"

"You need to chill. Time will tell you whether it's working or not."

I should try to chill and just take it as it comes. Jace has been single for a long time so I'm sure it's an adjustment on his part as well as mine.

I get back to my fresh bread while she is taking care of the pastries. She decided to prepare fewer quantities of our most popular items since we don't expect many customers to show up. The amount of snow outside is going to stop many of us from running errands. Tomorrow should be better once they cleared the roads and people felt like shoveling their way out to their car.

I'm closing shop with one strawberry shortcake left. The morning was terribly slow but the afternoon was great. I got many of my regular customers venturing out looking for something sweet. Most of them are in Christmas mode already and I'm starting the prep work for the holidays tomorrow. All my cakes are going to be Christmas themed. The hard work starts tomorrow whether we have more snow or not. This is the high season where I can't fail. It's tiring but so worth it.

"Boss lady, what's the plan for tomorrow?"

"We have a lot on our plate. We are operating with full staff too which means Felicity and Carla are in by 7:30. Christmas is just around the corner and we have to be ready. Snow or not, people have parties to attend or they are getting ready to host one. We got this."

"Of course, we do. We always do."

"Thanks for today. It means a lot that you came in and got things started for me."

"It's not every day I get a call from Mr. Jace King himself." She giggles.

"You are silly. I still can't believe he called you and let me sleep."

"I bet you needed it." She laughs.

I want to crawl under a table and hide but she's right, I so needed it. "Oh, please, stop." I laugh too.

Cecelia leaves the bakery laughing at me while I roll my eyes at her. "Whatever, girl."

I make a quick list of the priorities in the morning. Braided bread, Panettone, cinnamon star bread, etc. I have a lot to do and I'm looking forward to it. I think this Christmas will bring a new meaning to my life.

When it's time for me to leave, I sigh at the thought of not having any calls or text message from Jace. The best thing I can do is call him myself if I miss him that much or wait.

I like him a lot but I don't want to chase after him either.

Walking to my place, the sidewalk has been cleared of the snow and so was the entrance of my apartment. Sweet. No shoveling needed. I climb the stairs, unlock my door and walk through the door as I have been doing ever since I moved here.

There's something different this time, I step back and notice the Christmas wreath on my door with a tiny card and box. Of course I'm thrilled and I forget right away how much I missed Jace all day.

Walking back inside my place with both the card and box, I can't wait to open them. First I take off my jacket and boots and turn on the heat as chills run down my back.

I curl up on the couch with my thick leopard blanket and open the small envelope.

Bexley,

I'm sorry for all the trouble I caused you.

Derek

Well, that's bullshit. I throw the card on the floor as if it ruined my day. And in a way it has. What good can he give me in that box? Ridiculous. The box is way too tiny for all the things I wish he could give back. My whole life, for example.

I tear the paper wrapper with such anger that I might have torn the box too.

It looks like a jewelry box, one that I have seen before. It's the pink diamond earrings his grandmother gifted me on our wedding day. He knows I love them but I left them in the safe when I left. I had to cut ties in every way possible. Since the fire occurred, it hadn't even crossed my mind that I had still had belongings in the safe.

But...

Derek came here. He must have been the one who cleared my entrance. This is not okay. I get up again to check if my door is locked.

It is.

Shit. I don't feel unsafe around him but I do not want to be around him. It's pretty simple.

I'm surprised he was able to come here at all. That means he isn't in jail. I have no clue what the sentence of what he did could possibly be.

Now, I have to cook dinner and I don't feel like it. Yesterday's dishes are still lying on the counter. Ramen noodles might just be what I call a dinner tonight.

Or a grilled cheese. There is nothing like melted cheese and two extra buttery slices of bread. It's heaven in my mouth.

I get the ramen ready and throw it in the microwave while I take care of the grilled cheese. If I'm going to eat junk, I might as well do it right.

What I hate about ramen noodles is how good it smells because they are pretty much the opposite of healthy. Let's be real, it's terrible.

The card from Derek still has my blood boiling. How dare he come here?

"Unbelievable!"

I add a thick layer of butter to my bread slices and a mix of cheddar cheese and Monterrey Jack in the middle.

"That better be good."

As if it wouldn't be. I can't fool myself. It's cheese, what's not to like?

The only thing missing right now, is a TV. That would be great!

And Jace too. I mean, wherever he is right now, I hope he is okay.

I eat my emotions. That means both grilled cheese sandwich and ramen noodles are going directly down to my stomach. The holidays are just around the corner. It's my first Christmas as a divorced woman. It's hard. I'm happy to be starting a new chapter of my life but the status of being divorced weighs on me. It means I failed or we failed. I'm not sure. I'm proud that I got out of the marriage but I hate the title it gave me.

Once I'm done with what I call a dinner. I stab a fork in the leftover cake from last night.

Damn, Bex, stop eating and stop feeling this way. You had the best sex ever this morning. That means I'm supposed to have a smile glued on my face for at least a week... or until the next time.

To help my mood, I click play on a YouTube Christmas songs mix and get ready to clean up my mess. I start with the bullshit card I received which I throw in the trash but the earrings ... I'm keeping them. There's nothing wrong with that. His grandmother is the definition of a sweetheart and I've always loved her gift to me.

Dish after dish, I clean the kitchen and feel sick to my stomach for all the bad nutrition decisions I've made tonight. Maybe I shouldn't have eaten so much cake or everything. Too late for regrets now.

I sing along to pretty much all of the songs when suddenly my doorbell rings. Damnit.

"Hello, who is it?"

"Bexley, it's me."

Not Jace but Derek. "I'm with my sister. Can I come in? I mean no harm."

"Derek, you can't keep showing up like this."

"Please."

Groaning with frustration, I unlock on the door and let them in. The only reason why I'm allowing him in is because of his sister, Natalie. I'm pretty sure I can trust Natalie. When I started dating Derek, we became good friends and then, she met someone and our busy schedule made it hard to hang out anymore. I've always been there for her and her for me through the years but I kept the issues of my marriage under lock and key. She idolized her brother, and they were always very close.

"Hi Bex, sorry for just barging in here like this." Natalie says giving me a one armed hug before stepping back towards Derek.

I shrug. "Why are you here again?"

"I owe you an apology."

"Only one? You sure owe me more than one, Derek."

"I know but I came here wanting to talk about what happened yesterday. The bakery, the house and how I have involuntary included you in my problems. When I found out that you were with another man, I lost it."

"We are divorced. If I meet the right man, I might give it a try."

"It sounds like you have already met the right man."

"Derek." Natalie warns him.

"Fuck! I'm sorry. That's why I came here, to say that I'm sorry."

"Thank you but it doesn't mean your intrusions in my life are okay by any means. You have to stop that now."

"I love you, Bexie."

I shake my head. "No, you don't get to call me Bexie. Do you realize that I have spent years looking after you when you were drunk? Years... all the promises we had made to each other to start a family, be happy, taking care of each other, none of that happened. I cared for you 100% but I lost ten years of my life. Ten years I can't have back. That is the truth, how I feel right now. Instead of having kids running around the house like most couples do, I have an apartment by myself."

"I'm sorry."

"I know you are now, but being sorry now doesn't change anything." I breathe in. "I think it's best if you leave now and give me the space I deserve."

"Okay. Thank you for letting us come inside." Natalie says.

My words appear to have touched him. He looks broken, or hurt.

"I'm... I'm thankful for everything that you have done for me. I promise I'll keep my distance from now on."

I watch them leave my apartment speechlessly. The door closes and I'm left staring blankly at it. Will he go to jail for what he has done? I don't know and I didn't ask him either.

Still in shock that Derek showed up here with his sister, I sit on my couch and go through what was said. Maybe I was harsh with him, but we're divorced and it's too late to want me back. End of our story. I'm working on a new one now. Already.

Resting my head on the couch, I inhale deeply and exhale slowly. "This is fucked up but I can't let this ruin my day." I say out loud but I don't move an inch. It exhausted me to have to face him and Natalie. I wasn't mentally prepared.

The doorbell rings out again.

"What the hell? Is this some kind of a joke?" I say to myself as I get up and ready to open the door again.

I ask *who's this* praying it isn't Derek again, hoping it is Jace. Please.

"It's Jordan and Mitch from the fire station. We have something for you."

Yeah, okay, I know them. Jordan prefers extra icing on his cinnamon buns and Mitch loves cannolis.

"Okay, hold on a second."

I wonder what they want. Is Jace okay?

I unlock my door for the second time tonight and open it up for them.

"Everything okay? I ask wondering why they are carrying bags and a huge box.

"We came here for two reasons." Mitch says reaching my door first.

"Jace and half of our guys are out of town helping set up an emergency camp. An apartment building was completely destroyed last night and there are many families without a roof over their head tonight. Our guys are over there helping set up temporary shelters and making sure everyone has a bed to sleep on."

Oh. Well. That makes me feel like a spoiled brat. He is kicking butt somewhere around here to help people and I'm here missing him and wishing he would call.

"Do you know how long he will be there?"

"We don't, but in the meantime, he wanted us to bring over your brand new Christmas tree.

"And a shit load of ornaments. I think Jace is losing his freaking mind."

"We talked about having a tree. I guess he started planning it."

"Trust me, he did." Mitch puts the big rectangular box on the floor. "Now, I just want to ask you something."

"Sure." I say hesitantly.

"Jace is like a brother to me and I know how much he's falling for you, I just want to ask you if you are serious about this because he won't admit it to me but I'm sure he's already making some serious plans with you."

"I'm not playing him or using him as a rebound if that's what you are asking."

"Good. So, where do you want your Christmas tree?"

This is awkward.

"Uhh, by the window, right here."

This way, I can look at it from the kitchen or from the couch.

"Unless you want your tree to look like it spent the night at a rave party, I think you better do the decorating yourself." Mitch says.

Laughing, I nod. "That's fine with me."

"Okay, then. We'll see you around." Jordan says before giving me a quick hug.

"If Jace gets in touch with you, please tell him to call me."

"Bexley, if Jace has one call to make, it won't be to talk to us. I'm pretty sure you'll be the first person he'll call." Mitch explains with a gentle smile.

"Tell him to call us." Jordan teases.

"O-okay. Thanks guys."

They leave my apartment and I catch myself lost in my thoughts as I go through everything that they've just said. It's clear that Jace is very attached to me and I am to him just as much. Life is full of surprises. This is a good one, obviously.

Excited, I look through the bags of goodies and find tons of ornaments. Enough for at least two trees. I take what I prefer, turn on Christmas music and start adding joy to the tree.

I need to get him a Christmas present. I'm not sure exactly what, but I have to find something. I'll be too busy to go shopping so I'll simply have to find something online.

Maybe a frame, so he can add it to the empty walls of his place. He might like it since he wants to make his home feels like a home. Even better if he adds a picture of us. We don't have one yet. I must add that to our *to do* list.

What a change a year can bring! Last year, I was hiding the liquor bottles in hopes of having a decent Christmas but it didn't really help. Our tree had been the only decoration added to the house as I saw no point in being festive. I worked, I cleaned up the mess and went to bed, every single day. I don't miss the smell of beer or whiskey wafting in the bedroom as he came to bed.

So many sad memories. Letting go of everything like this was the best decision of my life.

He can try to ask for forgiveness but the bitterness in me isn't ready to let it go.

"Okay, enough about Derek." I breathe in and start adding ornaments to the tree again. Despite the bad memories, I'm back to smiling and filling the tree. It's sort of beautiful. Of course, it's mine. Ours.

I sit back down on my couch once I've added enough to the tree and stare at it for the longest time. Could it be happiness? Can it be that easy to be with someone? I'm starting to believe it could be.

I grab my iPad. I've got some shopping to do. First, I order myself a big flat screen TV, not as big as Jace's but one big enough that we can watch a movie together. I also add a few items for my favorite firefighter. This is the season, my time. I'm like a little girl again with a couple of wrinkles and stretch marks.

Chapter 8

If anyone says being a baker isn't a workout, I'll punch them. Maybe an uppercut.

Christmas makes people crazy and me as well. It's hard to keep up with the constant string of demands. As soon as I put the fresh buns or French baguettes out front, they disappear. I think the storm has made everyone late in their preparations and today is the day to catch up.

I haven't had time to catch up with Cecilia much. She is decorating cakes and cookies with Carla.

With my arms full of croissants in large plastic containers, I see my man striding up to the door. I almost drop everything and jump into his arms but instead he rushes to me to give me a hand.

"Wow, no need to take so many at a time." He then proceeds to grab all of them from my hands.

"Ten minutes and they'll all be gone. This season is out of control."

He puts the boxes on the shelf and then hugs the hell out of me. That moment makes me so happy. It's as if my whole body has come alive. My man is back and my day is made.

"I'm sorry for just disappearing like that."

"It's okay. You were helping people. That's what you do."

We are about to kiss but Cecelia calls my name and all eyes turn on me.

"Bexley, the cookies are out of the oven. You are welcome." She winks when she sees Jace standing next to me.

"I think we could use some help if you know what I mean." I smile all too widely at Jace trying not to be too obvious that I would love his help.

"I'll be happy to help. What can I do?"

"There are so many things you could do." I say laughing. "Aren't you working today?"

"I'm off for the holidays, two weeks."

I want to stick my tongue out at him, but I won't since I'm a mature adult. "Lucky you." He is and I'm definitely jealous.

"So, what can I help you with? Please keep in mind that I'm no baker."

"Don't worry, I'll find you something." I start walking toward the kitchen when I'm pulled back against his chest.

"Wait a second. Didn't you miss me a little?"

"A lot... sorry my brain is running at two hundred miles a minute. Thanks for coming and being here with me."

"I missed you too, Bex." He leans down to kiss me in front of the line customers. I don't mind at all but now, the rumors are going to spread like wildfire.

First, Derek crashing his car and the fire and now, I'm seen canoodling with the head firefighter. Oh lord!

"Hmm, Cecelia could use help with the cakes and cupcakes, they need to be wrapped and put in the cold room or you could get the cookies in their packaging. What do you feel the most comfortable with?"

"I don't think I can be trusted anywhere near the cupcakes so I'll deal with the cookies."

"Alright. I have to get the orange cranberry bread out of the oven and I'll have to help with the pies next. Follow me, hot stuff, I'll show you what to do." I smirk. The fact that he's here now with me, helping us means a lot. Who would rather work instead of relaxing at home during their time off? Jace King. Only Jace King.

"There are eight cookies per pack," I show him how to place the cookies, shut the plastic package. "Then, you seal it with the sticker."

"That's all? Can I at least do a quality check? I mean I'm all about quality control."

"You can have one." I giggle. "Just one."

"I'm 6'3", babe. I need at least two." Jace crosses his arms over his chest keeping a serious expression as he waits for me to give in. I know he isn't serious but his faux expression is funny as hell.

I take the package I have just wrapped and give it to him. "Here, Shrek, these are yours."

"Thank you." He laughs. "I love to see you smile."

"You are the reason I smile." A smile must be on my lips even when I'm asleep. I got a lot to deal with in my past but the future looks pretty amazing.

"Keep that smile on your face now." He jokes.

Gah! This isn't real. Apparently fairy tales exist and I'm only finding out today.

I leave him so he can eat his cookies and get started with his tasks.

I need to get focused; I have tons of things to do.

"Bexley, you have a delivery up front." Carla announces.

"Already? Wow that was fast." I don't know if it's the TV, the frames or both.

I hurry up to the front of the store only to see a really large box. "Where do I sign?"

"What is this?" Jace asks.

"A TV. I think it was time I got one, don't you think?"

"I was going to get you one for Christmas." He sighs.

"Too late. You are going to have to find something else."

Jace signs the paper to confirm delivery and takes care of moving the big box out of the way.

I hope I get the rest of the things in time. This was a sort of last minute thing.

Back to the list of things to do, it isn't as bad as I thought. Most things are under control. If I could, I would lock myself home with Jace for an entire week. It isn't possible yet but after the holiday rush, I intend to do just that. Hopefully I will be able to squeeze in a few days off.

As the afternoon comes and goes, my focus is on the baklava which I make only on demand. It's delicious but it takes forever to make. Every Christmas, I receive requests for it, sometimes for Easter as well.

The day flies by and it sucks. I wanted my day to last forever. Jace in my world having a good time is great. He makes working fun and I'm truly entertained by his passion for taste testing. Or the few pounds he is going to gain.

When the sun is out, the city is quiet and my energy level low, I walk home with hot bags of food from my favorite Chinese restaurant. Jace left the shop an hour ago to get to my place with the TV. I think it can count as a gift to him too. He was thrilled.

Happy to go home and finally relax with my man, I smile. If I could run home, I would but I don't feel like ruining dinner if I trip or slide on a patch of ice. The stairs up to my apartment are the death of me after a day of running around like a chicken with its head cut off. "Jace, can you give me a hand?" I say stepping inside.

The table is set, the cheerful Christmas lights warm up the room and my gorgeous Jace is walking toward me with a glass of wine.

"Take this, and I'll fix the plates."

He takes the food from my hand and gives me time to undress.

"What did you order? It's heavy."

"I ordered enough to have leftovers." I smile. "Leftovers make perfect lunch for the next day." I push my boots off of my feet and take my glass of wine.

"Right and we are going to need energy for tomorrow. Christmas Eve's got to be crazy for you at the bakery." He says bringing the food to the table.

"People come and get their orders, some come to empty my shelves at the last minute. There's enough of every type of people to where I have the ovens constantly going to keep up with the demand."

"I never thought it would be like this until today. I'm glad I could help you." He unwraps the egg rolls and places one on each of our plates.

"I'll need your bank information so that I can pay you."

He laughs out loud. "Hell no. I was there to spend time with you, not to make a few extra bucks."

I blush. "I loved having you with me today."

"I loved my day. It was a delicious type of day." He rubs his belly. "I can't believe I'm still hungry after everything I have eaten today. Quality control was done meticulously though."

"There is no way you could do that every day. You would be obese within a mouth."

"I have a good metabolism." He blinks. "Believe it or not, I'm starving so I would very much love to eat."

"Suit yourself. I'm starving too." I dip my egg roll into the sweet sauce and watch him devour his. "You barely had two bites. I would say a big one."

He nods unable to talk with his mouth full. "I told you I'm starving but the truth is I didn't eat much when I was away. So now, I could eat about anything in record time."

"They didn't feed you?"

He nods. "They did, but there were people around me that needed more. I only ate to keep my energy up. When you find yourself in a crisis like that, just days away from Christmas, it's hard. They have lost almost everything."

"Your heart is pure."

He shakes his head. "Nah, it isn't but I was more fortunate than them. I was able to go home to a refrigerator full of food, a warm bed, clean clothes, you know? For now, they've lost that and have to figure out where to go and what to do. Food is all they have to keep warm and feel better."

I nod and don't know what else to say. Starting over is hard, I know because I've been there but my situation wasn't exactly the same.

We eat more food, Jace eats a lot. I don't think there will be any leftovers for tomorrow when he is done. Meh, that's okay. I don't think I'll have time to eat anyway. Tomorrow will be insane. Customers will most likely be impatient, in a rush or feeling the holiday mood. Two opposites that I always deal with at this time of the year.

"Thank you for the Christmas tree. I was surprised to see Mitch and Jordan at my door but it's exactly what I needed. Derek and his sister had showed up unexpectedly only minutes before they did and..."

Jace puts his fork down. "Derek came here?"

I nod. "Yes, to say sorry. It took me by surprise, I didn't expect him to show up here. He was okay, I think I was the mean one."

"Well, I guess I'm happy that you were. I know he is your ex-husband but he messed up. It could have been a lot worse. He could have hurt someone when he got behind the wheel or when he burned the house down. It's…"

"Terrible, I know. I think he now realizes that we are really done and it's hard on him but I'm not going back."

He shakes his head. "Hell no, you aren't."

"I'm not and I made that clear. It's behind me, and I'm going forward."

He doesn't smile but I see happiness shine through his eyes.

"Enough of talk of Derek now, I want to enjoy my dinner."

"Of course."

Chapter 9

Christmas day.

Christmas Eve at the bakery was just as busy as I thought it would be and then some, but I had fun. Christmas music was playing a bit louder than usual and I might have danced my way from customer to customer. I had planned to close shop at 4 pm but it didn't happen before 6 pm. God! I had more customers this year than ever before. I'm glad Cecelia offered to stay late and help because I would have spent the evening prepping otherwise. When business is good, I'm happy. Everything is coming up roses lately.

Waking up, already exhausted, I rub my eyes and turn my head to the right where Mr. Firefighter is. He is still resting peacefully. I let him sleep and get out of the bed as quietly as possible.

It's Christmas after all. He deserves some extra sleep. I, on the other hand, only have a few hours to work at the bakery then I'm free for almost two days. TWO amazing days off.

I get dressed as fast as I can, drink some milk from the carton, get my keys and purse and I'm outta here. Today is easy and fun. As soon as I'm at the bakery, my only concern is the fresh breads and pastries. The cakes, buns, pies are already made and I'm just waiting for the people to come and get them.

Cecelia and the rest of the staff are off today, so it's just me here for a couple of hours.

Then it's back home, a nice Christmas dinner and spending some quality time with Jace. Just us. My family won't be coming this year. I'll try and see them in January. It's a first that I don't see Mom for the holidays. The timing was off this year. It happens. At least, I won't be by myself. I'm rather excited to spend the holidays with Jace. It'll be a fun and a new experience. No need to worry about how wasted or sick Jace will get, because he isn't like that. I expect a drama free day.

As I walk to the bakery, the sun is starting to rise. Shivers run down my back as the cold air hugs my cheeks and legs. I quicken my pace in hopes of getting to the bakery faster.

It's pretty quiet at this hour, everyone is still sleeping or getting ready to face the day. There are times like today where I miss my bed and wish I could sleep until noon.

But I can't. The bakery is my main source of income and I have to work and offer the best service possible. It's a choice I made when I became the owner.

When I finally get inside, I take a few minutes to eat breakfast. I break one of yesterday's French baguettes in half, get some chocolate spread and a warm and dark coffee. I look and feel tired. My eyes are still puffy and my hair well, let's just say I'm glad I'll be putting it in a ponytail under a net.

The shop will be opening its door within an hour and normally, there's a line of people waiting outside.

I get the oven ready for the bread and take care of cutting each loaf into evenly sized squares then I proceed with the shaping of the French baguette. This is the relaxing and fun part for me. I stretch the dough, add some flour and place them on the parchment paper. When the oven's ready, I place them on the center rack and move on to the next thing to do.

The front of the store needs to be ready for opening and on Christmas Day, it can get crazy in no time. Small knocks on the glass door make me jump like it's Friday 13th and I've just watched a marathon of Jason Voorhees.

"Holy shit." I say as I turn around and see Mr. Firefighter waving at me with a sheepish smile on his face. "You scared me." I say as I open the door for him. "What are you doing here? You should be sleeping."

"Well, I got a few things to do this morning and I wanted to see if you needed my help."

I lean my head to the side. Isn't he cute? "I think I'm okay but if you want to stay, I'm not going to kick you out."

With that said, he removes his jacket and gives me the biggest good morning hug ever.

"Sounds like a plan. I'll stay here for an hour or two. What were you doing just now?"

"Making sure everything is pretty and organized, you know?" I shrug, not knowing exactly what to say but I like my shop in order and pretty when the customers start rolling in.

I don't know what happened but that seems to really please Jace because he is rushing to me like a man with a mission. His strong arms and hands lift me off the floor and spin me around.

"Jace, what are you doing?" I giggle and hold on to him with all the strength within me.

"It's Christmas, we have to make the day extra special even if I'm tired as hell. This is it. The best time of the year."

"We still have birthdays and Easter or Valentine's Day."

"Just let me be happy for a minute." He says cheerfully.

Of course, I say to myself as I squeeze him harder. My lips leave a kiss on his neck as he puts me down.

"Merry Christmas, Bex."

Oh, okay. That simple. "Merry Christmas, Jace." I bite on my lip. "I've got to check on the French baguettes."

He nods, kisses me briefly and lets me go. "I'll make everything pretty over here."

Well, that will perk up the mood of my Christmas morning. Company is always nice. The doors are about to open and having him around even if it's just for thirty minutes or an hour will help. Less running around for me.

With my arms full of cupcakes, breads, buns and such, I cross the street to the firefighters in charge and leave them some of my overstock. I have been doing this every year. There's always too much for me to bring home and I know they'll eat every bit of it.

Just as I step out of the station, my phone starts to ring.

"Hello handsome." I say with a smile on my face. "Are you missing me yet?"

"Bex, every year, you give my guys your goodies. Thank you. I appreciate it."

"Wow, you have good source. I was there two seconds ago."

"I do. They call to make fun of me because I won't have any of it this year. That's the only downside of being on vacation."

"Don't worry, you'll have plenty of what they can't have. I'll be home soon."

Walking home in the middle of the day is awesome. It never happens on a regular day of work. I always work in the early morning to closing unless Cecelia volunteers to take the morning or closing shift. Jace will be home already so I'm planning on relaxing with him and plan a nice dinner. Of course, I didn't get a turkey or anything special for Christmas but I'm sure I can manage. Right? I have enough food at home and plenty of sweet desserts.

When I reach the stairs of my small apartment, the smell of food cooking makes my mouth water. "Oh my God!" Jace is cooking for us. I run to the top of the stairs and swing the door swiftly open startling Jace. "WOW! You scared the hell out of me."

Quite an amazing view greets me when I open the door. My handsome manly boyfriend is wearing my pink flowery apron and oven mitts. This is enough to make me pause and stare, trying to mentally assess the situation. I stifle a giggle and close the door behind me. "It smells so good in here, what are you doing?" I see pots, potatoes, crème and plenty of things laid out on my counter. It's hard to know what Jace is preparing.

"It's a secret."

I look at him with my are-you-kidding-me face. "Come on."

"Nope. Give me the dessert and take your jacket off."

I do as he says and I realize he isn't going to tell me. It's a surprise and that alone should make it all more interesting.

When was the last time I had a surprise on Christmas Day? I think it was Derek and I's first Christmas as a married couple. His sister came over to do my nails, my hair and make-up while he and his mom were planning dinner. Natalie had just graduated from beauty school at the time. It was fun. I remember how pretty I felt that day. Derek said I was. It went downhill after that. The Christmas after was the last one where my life still had a sense of normalcy. He still had some control and wasn't entirely drunk at the end of the night. I've always wondered what triggered him. Was it me? I... I don't know.

"Have you thought about the wishing well at all since that night?" Jace gets me back to us. Now. Present time.

"What do you mean?" I'm not sure I follow him.

"Your wish... well, my wish. I only asked for one wish and so far, it's positive. I think it's true what they say about the wishing well after all."

I frown. "You know we can't ever talk about our wish. It's supposed to be bad luck."

"Screw the bad luck, baby. I know what we have is real. It would've happened anyway but maybe the wishing well helped things along a little bit."

I giggle. It's hard not to fall for him when he's debating if he should or shouldn't believe the rumors of the wishing well of Hawkins.

"At least, now I know what you wished for." I say walking toward the living room.

Jace scoops me up into his arms before I can sit on the couch. "Tired?"

"Maybe. Well, I'm always tired this time of year." We sit closely on the couch. My head rests on his shoulder.

"I think you should hire more people or give more responsibilities to Cecelia. You open or close shop, but you can't do both. It's too much and you are going to end up sick or too exhausted to get up in the morning. I've seen it with some of the boys when they are burning the candle at both ends. It's rough."

"I know, but it's hard. I like what I do so it's extra hard to give away the hours. It's a responsibility I gladly took on when I bought the bakery, but I can admit that it's a lot of hours and having a little more freedom wouldn't be so bad sometimes."

Jace nods. "I know. We will figure it out."

I like how he says we. It shows his level of commitment.

Jace cares.

Jace doesn't want me sick.

Jace doesn't want me tired.

Jace wants me to enjoy more liberty.

Jace wants to spend time with me.

Derek didn't.

How can I explain that in the years I was with Derek, he never showed any sign of concern for my well-being, but Jace does after just days of us being together? Derek never took care of me the way Jace does.

It's heartbreaking in a way. Moving on from my life with Derek and not thinking about it is my only choice or it's going to haunt me and hurt me at every turn.

I cuddle closer to Jace and breathe in his cologne. He always smells so good. Fresh like laundry and strong nature or something. I haven't figured it out yet, but I'm hooked.

"Don't fall asleep on me now. I want to give you something."

I look up at him. "What? You got me something?"

He laughs. "Of course, I did, silly." He stretches out his arms to the small table next to the couch and grabs the square box in a red wrapping paper. "Here. I hope you like it."

I sit straight to take a better look at the gift. "Thank you. You shouldn't have."

He doesn't say anything but I know he's watching me.

I shake the box a little bit, not much appears to be moving in there. "I'm curious but I have no idea what it is."

"It's just something that I saw and I had to get it but I don't think you can guess it."

"It's heavy too."

I unwrap the box like a little kid, the excitement is there. It is always fun to get a gift, no matter what age you are. Under the paper, I find a brown box that doesn't give anything away. As I opened the box, I see it and it's the best gift he could have given me. A snow globe with the Hawkins wishing well. "This is the perfect gift. The night it all started. The wishes. It was a great night and now, I'll have this to remember the moment forever."

He leans closer and kisses my temple. "I was hoping you were going to like it. I have more presents for you but I'll keep them for later."

"I got you presents too but I don't think they will be quite as meaningful as this one. It really touches me." I shake the snow globe with my hands and watch the little snowflakes swirling around the wishing well. "Thank you." I say reaching for his lips. We kiss and it's soft, loving and perfect. The mood between us is relaxed and comfortable, so is our kissing. The Christmas tree softly illuminates the room and the music playing in the background keeps my heart warm. Everything about now is what I've always dreamed of.

"I love you, Jace." I say. It's a deep feeling I have started to adjust to. Love is strong, powerful. It's easy to get lost in, but with Jace, I'm sure he will hold my hand and guide me through it.

"I love you, Bexley."

I smile and tears appear in the corner of my eyes.

A surprise dinner is awaiting. One that I haven't cooked and it smells spectacular.

More presents are about to be exchanged.

I don't think I could ask for anything better than this. I'm the happiest I've ever been.

Sometimes it's the little things in life that make the biggest difference. I don't ask for diamonds or caviar, just a man who takes good care of me.

Just like Jace.

Life with him is a wish that came true.

If you enjoyed this tale, the best compliment you can pay the author is to leave a review where you purchased it, or tell a friend! Thank you for reading.

Jude Ouvrard is a mom, a girlfriend, a sister, and a daughter... well, you get the idea.

She's also an avid reader and writer. Ouvrard loves books—the words in them, and the worlds of fantasy they create. Basically, she's a sucker for any type of romance book. That's her thing.

Born and raised in a small village in the Canadian countryside, it's been nearly two decades since she moved out of the family home to go explore and enjoy the city life. Living with her longtime boyfriend, their son, and their fur babies in Montreal, her days are labored away at a law firm while she lives her dream job by night. Writing. Creating. Giving shape and form to the characters who whisper their stories in her head.

Ouvrard writes new adult, military, and contemporary romance tales filled with drama, love, and everything in between.

Also by Jude

- Under the sun
- Wonderland
- Lost Dreams
- Body, Ink, and Soul
- Music, Ink, and Love
- Ink me more
- Forever in Ink
- Inked Out
- Not Afraid to Love You
- Safe to Love You
- Beneath the Stars
- Ophelia
- Keep me warm
- Flawless
- Lost & Rich
- Sweetness
- Loving Sweetness
- January Part 1
- January Part 2
- River
- Bitter Dust
- Litthie White Lies
- Hidden Truths